OVER THERE

A HISTORICAL NOVEL

SALVATORE MAMONE

OVER THERE
A HISTORICAL NOVEL

iUniverse books may be ordered through booksellers or by contacting:

iUniverse
1663 Liberty Drive
Bloomington, IN 47403
www.iuniverse.com
844-349-9409

ISBN: 978-1-6632-6818-1 (sc)
ISBN: 978-1-6632-6819-8 (e)

Library of Congress Control Number: 2024922199

Print information available on the last page.

iUniverse rev. date: 10/26/2024

Over there, over there,

Send the word, send the word over there

That the Yanks are coming, the Yanks are coming

The drum's rum-tumming everywhere

So prepare, say a prayer,

Send the word, send the word to beware

We'll be over, we're coming over

And we won't come back till it's over, over there.

Chorus for *Over There* by George M. Cohen

This book is dedicated to my sister, LuAnn, who died too soon at 18. She did not live a full life because of the cancer that struck her.

I acknowledge my brother Vincent's, assistance in once again, proof reading this book to make it a better book to read.

This book takes place on two continents and England; to help the reader remember the characters, the author has created this cast list. I would recommend you make a copy of this cast list and keep it handy when reading.

CAST
Haskell Kansas
Margaret – mother, dies in chapter 1

Dr. Jonathan Guest – doctor in Haskell

Rebecca Guest – wife of Jonathan

Peter - son of Margaret and adopted by Dr. Jonathan and Rebecca

Sara – friend of Peter

Samuel, nick named Sam, a friend of Peter

Howard, a friend of Peter

Ida, mother of Howard

San Antonio Texas
George - son of Margaret and adopted by Jason and Monica

Jason – San Antonio School teacher

Leonard Jones– a friend of young George

Juan Ortiz- a friend of young George

Steven brother of Juan

Jose brother of Juan

Monica wife of Jason – part time book keeper

Mark – father to Leonard and bank manager

Michael – mother to Leonard and stay at home mom

Savana – George's friend

Brest France
Jack Montague - Brest France dock worker

Marie -wife of Jack

Marie – daughter of Jack and Marie

Piere -son of Jack and Marie

Jack son of Jack and Marie

Patrica alias Pat friend of Jack

Father John – parish priest

Seaforth, England

Andrew Wallace dock worker at Seaforth, England

Alexander son of Andrew

Susan wife of Andrew

Archie son of Andrew

Amanda friend of Archie

Michael friend of Archie

Mathew Friend of Archie

Mary Mother of Mathew

Bridget girlfriend of Mathew

Braunau am Inn in Astria-Hungry

Noah Wagner Son

Rachael Wagner Mother

Otto Wagner Father

Nora friend of Noah

INTRODUCTION

This book is called a *Historical Novel* because it includes historical people, such as, Truman, Pattan, Persing, and others. It also includes actual battles and actions such as, The Russan Revolution, which had a major impact on the World War and history.

Extensive research was done to make this book reasonably accurate [see reference at end].

PART 1

Turn of the Century

CHAPTER 1

Haskell, County December 31, 1899

The doctor was not sure that he could save either child, but he knew that he could not save the mother. Margaret was a very small woman with corresponding small hips. This was making a normal delivery impossible. Even with the single bare light overhead the doctor could see how hard Margaret was fighting to deliver her soon to be born sons. Margaret was an unwed mother who ran away from home to have her child. Her mother pleaded with her to "get rid of the problem" but Margaret would not give up the only thing that would ever truly love her. It would cause her death. The father, an older man who promised to "Always love her," disappeared and went back to his wife as soon as Margaret told him the news. With no money at home and her mother worried what others would say, Margaret had no choice but to leave home and fend for herself. And now, on the last day of 1899, with the world celebrating a new century, Margaret would give birth to twin boys she would not ever see.

Margaret was in labor for hours. This was due to her small size, the lack of equipment at the small doctor's office, and medical care in those days. The bed was wet with her perspiration, sweat, and blood. Finally, after 10 hours, the doctor could not stand to see Margaret in any more pain and he opened her up to save the child. He was not surprised that Margaret did not survive the operation, few did in those days, but he was surprised to find that there were two boys and not one.

"Margaret, you have two beautiful sons. I wish you could see them," he said.

"I did everything I could for you but it was not enough. But I promise I will make sure your sons are well taken care of."

And then the doctor cried over the still warm but becoming cold body of Margaret Hand.

At almost the stroke of midnight, with a new century to be celebrated, and with limited funds, Doctor Guest buried Margaret in a small plot outside the local church in Haskell County Kansas. It wasn't much but then Margaret never had much in her short life so it was fitting that she should be buried in a simple pine box coffin and in a simple plot. Doctor Guest hoped her children would have a better life.

CHAPTER 2

Haskell County 1/1/1900

After the difficult night he had it was no wonder that Doctor Guest slept for nine hours. The new additions to his household, George and Peter were beautiful babies. Doctor Guest had named them with names that he would have used for his own sons if he had ever had any sons that were born alive and not dead. They were definitely twins because you could not tell them apart. If you looked very carefully you could see a very small mark on Peter's chest; a mark that George did not have. The mark was the size of a pin head and if you looked closely it looked like a heart. As Peter grew, so would the mark but unless you took their shirts off you would not be able to tell them apart.

"Jonathan, what will we do with the children?" asked his wife, Rebecca.

"I am not sure," he said. "What do you think about keeping them for ourselves?" he replied.

"Jonathan, you know that we can't handle children at our age."

"I know, I know. It was just a thought. But they are so beautiful, how can I just give them away to a home?"

"And what home do you have in mind? Or what church? This is not a big town you know."

Jonathan thought about this for a moment. He wanted the children to stay with him. Even though he and Rebecca were past middle aged they could still give the children a home. It would be better than a large home for foster children. Those places were hardly any better than the homes in Oliver Twist. Jonathan tried to think if he knew anyone in town that could give the children a home but the town was so small and the people in general were almost as old as he was. It was almost as if the town was aging with them. Young couples were moving out and no new people were moving in.

"Rebecca, what if I can find a home for only one child? What would we do with the other child?" he asked.

"I think the best idea is to find one home and keep them together. They are brothers and they belong together."

"I agree, but I am just asking." But after a night of restless sleep Johnatan had an idea. Johnatan had a friend who lived in a small town near San Antonio, Texas and loved children. He and his wife had two children who died at an early age, one from measles and the other by an accident. They might be willing to start a new family. The other child Johnaton would keep. He always wanted a son and this was a way to get one.

CHAPTER 3

Brest France 1/1/1900

Marie was only one year old and already she was able to say a few words. The fact that the words were in French made that even more impressive. This was 1900 and the beginning of a new century and her mother and father had high hopes for her; she would not be a seaman's wife if they could help it. She would marry an important man and leave the ships to others. She would leave this small town and move to an important city. She would have beautiful happy children and live in a fancy house. There are several rich families because Brest was a major deep water port city with many cargo ships coming and going. Several families have responsivity for all the companies that handle the docks and the cargo coming and going.

The Montague family lived in Brest, France a peaceful town on the west of Franch. Brest had one of the best deep-water seaports on the cost of Europe. Because of it's deep port, large ships were able to dock large cargo ships. Because of the number of ships, the town also had several service spots such as restaurants and a hotel, gas stations and more. Shipping is a very important revenue maker for Brest. With the friction in Europe the port at Brest would be important for ships caring soldier from America to disembark; if America entered the war.

The Montague family consisted of a father, Jack, mother Marie, like her mother and now her daughter, and two sons Piere and Jack like his father. The boys were born 16 months apart and were now 7 and 5 years old, old enough to be given a sip of champaign to celebrate the new year and century. They were also old enough to be a good help at home even just to clean up and make some pocket money from their allowance.

5

The boys were born soon after their young mother was married. The daughter was an after though that came after a Christmas party with too much to drink.

It was a happy family but with trouble in Europe the parents were afraid that the problems could affect France and their two boys. With the big ports at Brest, it was sure to affect their town.

CHAPTER 4

San Antonio, Texas 1/2/1900

Jonathan contacted his friends Jason and his wife Monica regarding the boys and would they be willing to take George as their son. Jonathan's wife could hear the yell across the room as they said "yes". Jonathan knows Jason for years when they were the only two boys in their town that went to their local high school. When they finished school they went different ways, Jonathan to med school and Jasion to college to become a teacher. Jason became a grade school teacher in a large school and Monica was a part time book keeper and house wife. They would make excellent parents.

Before they could leave to pick up their mew son, and they liked to say son, they had to dig out the furniture they used for their other sons, buy food for the baby, and do other things to prepare the house for the new arrival. After they lost their sons, they hoped that one day they could use the furniture again and they are glad that they saved it.

Their comfortable three-bedroom, two-bathroom house is just the right size for the new addition. There is also a nice size back yard that George will be able to play in. It is an ideal house and community to live in.

Jason and his wife took a train to renew their friendship again and to take George home to Texas. With a school teacher as a father, he will get a good education.

CHAPTER 5

─⊹─ ⚙ ─⊹─

Haskell County 1/5/1900

The new century has the begging of friction in Europe. There was no fighting but it seemed that just a small incident could set Europe on fire. Both Rebecca and Jonathan hope that the troubles in Europe stop before America gets involved and Peter is called to fight. Peter is not old enough to fight now, he is only a baby as is George, but if the problems in Europe keep growing, they could be.

Jason and Monica arrived on January the fifth to see their new son. They came as soon as they could because they just could not believe they were going to be a family again. The two couples were happy to see each other after so many years. After they saw George and held him they talked about what they had been doing after so many years then they got to the real reason for the trip. George. They wanted to know where he came from and about his brother, Peter. They would love to take both of them bur Jonathan wanted a son of his own. Both families were perfect families for adoption and both were happy to be whole.

Jason and Monica only stayed one day because they wanted to set George up in his new room. When they left for the train station it was both happy and sad parting. Happy because Jason and Monica were leaving with their son, and sad because Jonathan was losing a son.

CHAPTER 6

Seaforth, England 3/5/1900

Seaforth was a port on the west side of England. Besides the port, it had a military presence with the Seaforth Highlanders. The port could not handle large cargo ships but it could handle many ships. Enough cargo arrived and left that the port needed a large staff to handle the work load, and it had the staff.

Andrew Wallace worked at the port and lived just outside the port with his wife Susan and his two young sons, Alexander age 5, and Archie.\ age7. They could not afford a house but they have a nice two-bedroom apartment that Susan keeps clean. Unless the boys can finish high school, they will probably have to work on the docks like their father. Andrew always wanted a daughter to play with but instead he had two fine sons. Maybe one of his sons can marry a nice Scotches girl and she produces a girl; he will have to be satisfied with his two fine sons.

CHAPTER 7

Brest France 3/1/1900

Marie was still one but she looks older. She is very pretty and her vocabulary is growing. She is going to be a very beautiful and smart young girl. The friction in Europe was growing and so were Marie's brothers. Nobody in the family wanted war or to have the two boys join the fight. People in Europe were wondering if war came would America help. The papers in Europe and America were filled with ominous articles about how bad a war would be. No one wanted a war but most people felt that one would evenly come and it would be a World War.

Like most men in Brest, Jack worked on the dock loading and unloading cargo. Marie worked in a restaurant but her daughter was too young to go to school and she did not have anyone to care for her so she had to give up her day job for a while. They were a happy family and they wanted to stay that way, without war.

The two boys in the family were just like other boys their age; happy, play full, and two young to worry about war or girls. Jack however, did have a friend, Patrica nicknamed Pat 6, who was one year younger than Jack was and they were good friends. She liked to play baseball and she was just as good as the boys. She did have dinner at times with Jack and she was glad for that because Marie was an excellent cook. Pat wanted to be a nurse when she grows up; she could not be a doctor because women do not become doctors and because there was no money for college so, she would be happy to be a nurse.

CHAPTER 8

San Antonio, Texas 12/25/1900

This was George's first Christmas and Jason and Monica found the best Christmas tree they could find and then took out the decorations that had not been used since their children had passed. Now they had a reason to celebrate again. Texas was mainly a Babtist state but they celebrate Christmas like most people. With an average temperature of 41 degree in December and very little snow during winter there is little hope for a white Christman for George.

Jason and Monica both gave a nice present and a stocking stuffer to each other. Jason received an expensive pen and new socks and Monica received a nice necklace and a coupon for a hair styling. Monica came out ahead as she usually did. The main gifts were for George. Jason and Monica went overboard with toys, new clothes, and a rocking horse, perfect for someone from Texas. Jason and Monica have never been happier, now that they have George. He was a happy baby who rarely cried and they knew, he would have a happy life.

CHAPTER 9

Haskell, County 12/25/1900

It is going to be a white Christmas in Kansas. Haskell has a white Christmas at least 20% of the time. It is going to be one of the best Christmas that Jonathan and Rebecca have had in a long time because now, they had Peter. They had not put up a tree for a while because it was too much trouble and because they were always busy but, this year they gave Peter a tree with all the decorations. They did not usually give gifts to each other because as Rebecca said "they have everything" but, this year they really do have everything, Peter. Peter is almost one year old so he cannot have many kinds of toys yet but, there were plenty of toys and gifts he could have and his parents bought him as many as they could find.

Winter always brought a rash of colds but, for some reason this year the colds were worse than usual. So far winter this year is worse than usual especially because it is so early in winter. It is colder than usual with more snow than usual, that could be the reason for the extra influx of patients. There was not much you could do about a cold except stay warm, drink fluids and yes, eat chicken soup. This year that did not help, and people did die from the cold. And winter had just started and it will get worse. The weather man claimed that it may be the coldest winter that the area has had for many years; that means there would be more patients for the doctor and more work keeping the house clean.

CHAPTER 10

───── ❀ ─────

Seaforth, England 12/25/1900

Like most of the world, England celebrates Christmas. They celebrate the same way with decorations, a tree, gifts, cards, and some things unique to the UK; regarding the celebration, from wearing crowns on your head to eating little mince pies. In the Andrew Wallace house, they have a tradition of each member painting a store bough decoration and putting them on the tree. After seven years the tree is full of decorations.

This year is different because it is the first Christman in a new century. People are doing more visiting to friends and neighbors. The port has many lights that will stay up till January 2; like most people and places they include New Year in the holiday season and when New Year Day is over it really is the end of the old and start of the new year.

Every body in the family received gifts that they could use and that made them happy. The boys received clothes and only one toy as a gift, and they were happy to receive the gifts because the family was not rich. When the boys get a little older, they can work and buy their own gifts.

CHAPTER 11

─────── ✳ ───────

Brest Franch 12/25/1900

The Brest port was decorated for the holiday from December 1 to January 6th. January 6th was celebrated as Christman in some households because January 6th was Epiphany, the day when the wise men gave gifts to the baby Jesus.

The boys each wanted a BB gun as gifts. Jack did not see a reason why they could not have a gun but, Marie said "no." With the boys pleading she finally gave in. Jack and Marie gave practical gifts such as work clothes for Jack and a new dress for Marie to wear on the few days that go out. The baby got new clothes and lots of toys, as expected for a baby. As usual the family had a wonderful lunch of roast duck, various vegetables, and wine, which this year Jack gave a sip to his boys and to top it off, orange cake.

The family was Catholic and on this. day they went to mass. They went to an old church where their daughter and their sons were baptized. Their priest, Father John, was a jovial 45-year-old man who was well loved by the members of the parish. One reason that they liked him was because he gave easy penance another reason was because he loved the young children and he could always make them laugh.

The port was busier than usually. A lot of cargo from America was arriving to Europe. People and countries are stocking up with all kinds of goods including military in case things start to lead to a war. Both boys are too young to work and thankfully to fight but, things could become worse and they would be asked to help in any way that they could.

CHAPTER 12

─── ❋ ───

Seaforth, England 12/26/1900

The UK has several holidays that other counties do not; one such holiday is Boxing Day. Boxing Day is the day after Christmas. Boxing Day was once a day to donate gifts to those in need, but it has evolved to become a part of Christmas festivities, with many people choosing to shop for deals on Boxing Day. Boxing Day is not always celebrated on the day after Christmas because it needs to be celebrated on a weekday, so, it does not always come on December 26.

The Wallace family do some shopping on the holiday but, they also stay home and enjoy their gifts. The family was not very religious but, for Christmas they do go to church. For Boxing Day this year, they decided as a treat, to have lunch at a local restaurant The restaurant was not fancy but, it give Susan a chance to be free from cooking.

CHAPTER 13

Braunau am Inn in Austria-Hungry 1/25/1900

Austria-Hungry as well as Germany, celebrate Christman the same as other Christians. They had a tree and decorations and singing carols and gift giving. Otto Wagner had a good job so he could afford nice gifts for his only son, Noah who was six, and Otto's wife Rachael. He could take his small family to a nice dinner but Rachael liked to cook so, instead, they ate at home with several neighbor friends who liked her cooking. Because of where they lived, the discussion was about any possibility of a war. As much as they disliked the Serbs, they still did not want a war that might cause them to lose their only son in battle. Winter in this area was cold and snowy so Noah had another white Christmas.

Noah did not have many friends but he did have Nora. Noah was 6 and so was Nora and they are in the same class at the local school. Neither knew what they wanted to do except they both wanted to go to high school. Nora was thinking about becoming a teacher but Noah liked math so he might be an engineer. Time will tell.

CHAPTER 14

─────── ❁ ───────

Haskell County 1/3/1901

Peter was growing up fast; he was now one year old. He was a quiet and well-behaved child. Eventually he would be eligible to enter pre-k class and learn how to make friends, learn some social skills and, and learn some basic subjects.

In those days people rarely went to high school and stopped their education, if lucky, at 8th grade. Dr. Guest wanted his son to get a higher education, maybe going to college and be a doctor like him. Jonathan would like to see Peter wearing a cap and gown but Jonathan is getting too old to live to see that. His wife, Rebecca, is aging faster than him, but she was older than him when they married. Even with her age, 67, Rebecca keeps a clean house, and cooks a well-balanced meal that helps the family keep healthy. When Peter starts school, he will give him extra training at home and when old enough he will teach him some basic medicine. He will be a big help in the office.

The office has been busy with measle patients. There was an epidemic and with no vaccine many people across the county were getting the measles and some were dying. It is expected that a million people will get this virus this year in America with up to 30% dying, especial children, and up to 1% of the population in America would die from the disease. There was very little Jonathan could do to treat the disease but he can try to protect his wife and child from catching it. It is well known that it is very easily spread so he is keeping Peter in his own room and Rebecca away from the exam room as much as possible. They both washed many times a day, especially after they examine a patient but he did not know if that helped. Doctors do often catch what their patient has so he is careful and is keeping away from Peter. Measles is a highly contagious, infectious disease caused by measles virus. Symptoms usually develop 10–12 days after exposure to an infected person and last 7–10 days. Initial symptoms typically include fever, often greater than 40 °C (104 °F), cough, runny nose, and inflamed eyes. With no vaccine there was very little that can be done except stay away from any one that has the disease because it was so contagious.

It hurts to be touched and people get delirious. There are mahogany spots on cheek bones, and then turn blue. Blood carries oxygen in arteries is bright red, without oxygen it is blue. The entire body could turn blue giving the impression of Black Death. Lungs chocked with blood. Blood poured from noses, ears, eye sockets and people had delirium. It was an ugly sickness to get.

CHAPTER 15

Seaforth, England 2/4/1903

Alexander and Archie are now 8 and 10 and a big help around the apartment by keeping their one room clean. They had a lot of friends, both male and female. The families of the kids were also friendly. Two girls, were very friendly with Archie, Michael, and Amanda. They were both one year older than Archie and were interested in him. Archie was not what you would call handsome but cute instead. He was his size for his age and not tall. People like him for different reason but all people say that he has a sense of humor.

People in England were just as afraid of a possible war as the people in Europe, but because they were an island they felt that they had some protection; but because of treaties their sons would still be required to fight in Europe. The crazy part is that the English do not hate the Germanies but would still be obliged to fight because of treaties with Franch. Alexander and Archie do not worry about the war they just worry about the exams that are coming up.

CHAPTER 16

Haskell, County 7/4/1903

It was the fourth of July in Haskell and as usual there will be a fire works display at the fairgrounds. It was not a professional display but for a small county it was just right with the right number of fireworks and noise. This was the first year that Peter was being taken to the display and Jonathan did not know if Peter would be afraid of the noise and lights in the sky. They did not bring food for Peter because they felt that Peter might be too excited or nervous to eat but they did bring milk for later. As usual, the fairgrounds were crowded with all the kids looking to the sky and covering their ears from the noise. Some people wore a large handkerchief to cover the mouth and nose. They did not know if that would help prevent getting the measles but it was better than nothing. Peter wanted the food that they did not take so, they gave him part of theirs. It was a great day and Peter would remember it and he would experience the noise and fireworks later in life.

CHAPTER 17

Haskell, County 9/4/1903

There were not many children Peter's age,3 so, he will not have many kids to play with when he is older. Sara, who Peter plays with so, he at least has one friend. There are two more boys who are one year older than him and they can probably become friends, when they get older

One is Samual nicknamed Sam. His family emigrated from Russia and had Sam in 2001, so he is one year older than Peter. His family consist of the mother and father and two sisters who were born in the late last century, in Russia.

Howard was the other young boy. He was almost the exact age as Peter, being born three days later than Peter. His family would have been large but the mother Ida, lost two children in child birth and can not have any more kids. The family is small but they are happy.

CHAPTER 18

Haskell, County 8/10/1903

Sara lived in a large house near Peter's house, so it was easy for them to become friends. The parents of both Sara and Peter know each other and they were the patients of the doctor. Sara and Peter were both three so there was little they could do but run around in the yard. There was a small swing that had two seats and it was just made for small children if someone was watching. Haskell was a nice place and kids are having fun growing up there. Because they are the same age, they could be entering school at the same time. They also must be careful of catching the measles and spreading it to the other kids.

The first three years of Peter's life went by fast, too fast for his parents. The parents knew that the years had many bad things, such as measles, and good things such as playing with Peter. Even though the doctor was always busy, he still made time to take Peter to see the town, sometimes with his friend Sara. They were beginning to be very close friends and it will be interesting to see them grow up together.

Sam and Howard were young and they sometimes visited Peter and Saera in the playground. The four of them were becoming a "click" and would be good friends as they grow older.

CHAPTER 19

—✦— ❁ —✦—

Brest Franch 10/9/1903

Jack was 10 now and his brother was 8; too young to worry about a war but, not too young for their parents to worry. Life in Brest was very busy; with more and more goods coming from America. Americans felt that is the best way that they could help their friends, England, and France, if there was a war. America was very strongly antiwar and sending troops to fight in a "Foreign War." Things were about the same with the friction between countries but, it can heat up at any time. Life went on as usual but, people still prayed for peace.

Jack and Piere still went to school and Jack helped in the office at home with light moving of equipment but Piere was still too young to lift the heavy boxes. Piere instead helped cleaning and learning to cook. With his help his mother was able to go back to work. Marie was four now and much easier to take care of. Next year she will be eligible for pre-k school and that will make her mother's life easier. With all the good things happening to the family, they were happy and did not think about a possible war. The different countries in dispute would sometimes be angry and other times be indifferent; no one would know if they would finally come to their senses and make peace.

CHAPTER 20

―――― ❀ ――――

Brest Franch 12/25/1903

Fater John decorated the church with a tree that is growing outside in the small yard and with decorations that the parishioners made over the years. The decorations also had a hand made and painted manger and figures. Last night was the midnight mass and this morning will be the 10 o'clock Christmas mass, which is usually packed. He took time out to visit a small nearby fort to say a mass with the soldiers. He always comes to the fort on Monday to hear confession and distribute the host. He is the only priest in the church and he was always tired. If there is a war and he serves with the troops, he does not know who will take care of his parish. He could not take off and go with the troops, he would need permission from the bishop and with a shortage of priests that might not happen.

Besides mass and confessions, he helps with the sick, and, there are many of them and not enough doctors to care for them, so he tries to help. His day is always full but, that is the way of a true priest.

CHAPTER 21

Brest Franch 11/15/1903

Pat, Jack's friend, and school mate comes from a small family. She was an only child and she was treated as such. She was well cared for. Her father works at the pier, like 89% of the men in town; the rest were too old or weak to work. Her mother also worked in the hardware store selling all kings of tools and other such goods. Pat was 11 years old and was showing interest in boys, particularly Jack. At his age Jack did not show that kind of interest in Pat but, when she grows bumps on her chest, he will.

Jack's parents have noticed Pat's interest with Jack and they are happy with that because they are good friends with Pat's parents. It is too early to be making wedding plans but if it happens, they will be very happy. Of course, being in Franch they know if there is a war, France will be attacked.

CHAPTER 22

Seaforth, England t/5/1905

The newspaper's main story was the possibility of a war. The government was suggesting that each large city form a tent city in a park and have eligible males practice things that would need to know if the war came to Europe. Seaforth was not large but because of the port they might need to learn how to protect the ships that dock there.

England's major military capability was it's navy. Because England was an island, they had lots of ports and ships to protect as well as the country to protect. The navy might be best for defense but the war will be fought on land.

Alexander and Archie were too young to go to a tent city and learn to fight but they were not too young to be curious about the tent city. The two of them went to the tent city, along with several more people their age as well as Michael and Amanda and a new friend Mathew who was the same age as Archie.

The tent city contained a dozen tents that could each hold about 30 people just enough to help spread the flu. Many men (100's of 1,000) were living in tents during these cold winters. Students 17 and 18 were taught some basic military stuff in high school; things such as how to march and salute and hold a rifle.

CHAPTER 23

Braunau am Inn in Austria-Hungry 1/5/1905

It is the start of winter and as expected it is cold and snowy. Unlike many people, Noah loved the winter. It was not the cold but the snow. He and Nora liked to make snowmen and snow angels and then watch them melt if it gets warmer. Christmas was nice and fun with lots of gifts for everyone. Business was good and with the cold weather most work will be inside to fix pipes that leaked with the cold weather. Those are easy jobs but paid well. Noah sometimes goes with his father to learn the trade so that he could have a good job for after high school. Life was good in the Wagner home.

CHAPTER 24

Haskell County 1/5/1905

Peter was five and was growing up fast. He was doing well in his pre-k class. There was no war in Europe but there was a lot of talking back and forth about a possible war. The main problem was between Serbia and Germany. Both sides had their allies which was good and bad. Good because they had more soldiers, bad because the other side had more soldiers. It was also bad because neither side had heavy military equipment except canons, the tank came later. They fought with rifles and many men died trying to get close to the other side. The casualties were going to be in the thousands for each side for each battle.

Peter was very young and there was no way this friction could continue long enough for him to enter the service. There were other things to worry about. Like the measles. The measles was all over the world and estimates are for 1 million people in America to catch the virus. Many people covered their mouth and nose with a small towel or large hankies for protection but no one knew if that helped.

There were articles in all the newspapers about troubles in Europe and what should America do if war came. It seemed so far away. Almost all families did not want to send their sons to war; and there was a rumor that girls wanted to go to be nurses and see the excitement. If families did not want their sons to go, they surely did not want their daughters to go. Women felt that they could help in hospitals and patching up the wounded. They also felt that they would be able to see Europe. Their parents felt otherwise.

CHAPTER 25

— ❋ —

San Antonio, Texas 1/1/1906

Because George was born at midnight it was difficult to determine which day he was born on and what day he should celebrate his birthday and what day should be his birthday.

Jason and Monica threw a fun filled party to celebrate their son's sixth birthday. Most of his classmates were invited and came, because George was very popular in class. George had started school this past September and he was making friends with the boys and the girls. Even at his age, girls would giggle when they saw him; he is going to have a line of girlfriends when he gets older.

George had started to ride a horse, as all young Texans did. There are lots of things that he is learning to do because he is a Texan. Like any male Texan, Jason bought George a BB gun for his birthday and he will teach his son how to shoot.

George had two close friends who were in a higher class; one was a small Spanish speaking boy named Juan Ortiz; the other was a tall, for his age, blond boy named Leonard Jones. Both Juan and Leonard were a year older than George but they still managed to be friends. As young boys they did all the young boy things and played games that are played all over. All three of them plus others loved baseball and they were all interested in the new thing called airplane. They would all go to the air show with George's parents. First sight of the strange airplane and then saw them fly put George and Leonard in love with the contraption and they wanted to fly one day.

CHAPTER 26

San Antonio, Texas 1/1/1906

Juan Ortiz was a member of a large family that consisted of two daughters and besides Juan, two other sons, one named Steven, for Saint Steven, and Jose, after his grandfather. They lived in a large rental house that was always kept clean. Juan was the second oldest child in the family but, the tallest. He did have a mild case of the measles which he transferred to the others in the family. He was doing well in class but he could not go to college because the family did not have the money. He loved math so he would probably become a book keeper like his father when he gets older. The family is happy and well loved and good citizens. If war comes to America they will be prepared to fight. Nobody in the family wants to go to war but, they will train and fight if they are told they must.

CHAPTER 27

Braunau am Inn in Austria-Hungry 5/5/1906

It is spring already but if was still as cold as winter could be. Business is busy because winter pipes may freeze and need to be replaced and that can be a large job that is difficult to do when it is still freezing. Noah has started to work with his father learning what tools are used for what job.

Rachael was a decent cook and liked to cook hardy meals for the two men in her life. The apartment that they lived in was just the right size for the three of them, two bedrooms and one bathroom. With Otto's good job he could afford more nut there was no need.

Noah is 12 and loves playing soccer or football as it is called in Europe. Noah has a school mate, Nora who is his same age and helps him with a French class. Life is good for both families. No one is thinking about the Serbs.

CHAPTER 28

San Antonio, Texas 1/1/1906 start

Leonard was an only child and as such was treated like a king by his parents. The father, Mark was a bank manager and made a nice salary. The mother, Michael, was a stay-at-home mom that took good care to her family and house. She always had a clean and neat house because they often entertained. Leonard had two good male friends and several female friends but, he did spend more time with the girls than you would expect from a seven-year-old boy.

Michael noticed that Leonard spent more time with the girls in his class. She was not sure why, and she felt that maybe she should talk to a doctor about the issue. She had no problem if he was gay, but other people might; this is Texas in 1906 after all.

CHAPTER 29

Seaforth, England t/5/1905

Mathew is in a single parent family. His father, John was killed while working on the docks, a common problem when working with heavy boxes of goods. His mother, Mary worked in a restaurant, six days a week as a cook. She was allowed to bring food home so she could help feed her and Mathew. They both missed John because he was a good worker and husband. Mary was still young enough and pretty enough to marry again but, with her long hours and taking care of Mathew she did not have the time or effort to meet anyone. Mathew had several friends that he played with so he was happy.

Some of the young kids that he plays with included Andrew, his brother Archie, and Bridget play and went to school together and even their families were close, so no one was thinking about war.

CHAPTER 30

Seaforth, England 6/8/1907

The ports were busier than usual because more goods were coming from America. Using the western ports of England would be an easier trip but with so many ships coming across the pond the ports on the eastern part of England had to be used for the smaller cargo ships.

Because this was England their favorite sport was socker or as it is known in England, football. The family and other kids would sometimes go to cheer on the local team and sometimes they went to a park to kick the ball around. It was a great life for the families, so far.

The army training camps have been in use for months and every trainee was there for three months service. They were training to shoot using American rifles such as the Springfield 1903-30-06 This was a good rifle and was also used by America later in the war. By staying in a camp, such as this one, for three months, the men got a feel for what the war would be like. The food served would be similar as what they would eat in the trenches, sometimes served cold just as it would be in the trenches. It was a good program and probably saved some lives.

CHAPTER 31

Brest, France 7/14/1908

Today is a special day in France, Bastille Day. July 14th or French National Day is the national holiday of France. There are traditions include a military parade in Paris and an aircraft flyover. This day in France is like July 4th in America. The day is celebrated all over Franch with fireworks, singing and dancing.

French National Day is the anniversary of the Storming of the Bastille on July 14th, 1789. That date was a main event in the French Revolution that celebrated the unity of the Frence people on 14 July 1790. Celebrations are held throughout France.

Marie and her family, like all families in France, celebrated July 14th by having parties, eating special food, and drinking. Since it is a holiday most people in Franch did not go to work to enjoy the holiday. The port, however, was still open which meant that most people in Brest had to work.

CHAPTER 32

San Antonio 7/12/1908

The news from Europe was not good. Different countries would be angry to others and nobody was trying to tone down the rhetoric. Every body felt for sure that there would ne a war, a war that no one wanted. George was only eight so, he was way too young to be enlisted but wars can last.

The talk in America by everyone, is if there is a war to stay out. British and French people hoped that there was no war but, they hoped that America would help. The best thing that England and France can do to avoid a war was to stay out. Because of treaties saying out is not possible.

George was eight now and he is becoming a fine rider. He was almost good enough to ride in a rodeo but he was too young for that. He is doing well in class and more popular with the girls. His parents wondered how his twin was doing and if he felt that he should let George know that he had a brother but they decided not to do that until he is ready to know the truth.

CHAPTER 33

— ❋ —

Brest Franch 9/12/1908

Friction was becoming worse in Europe and war seemed more likely every day. Countries were all rearming and asking young men to enlist now so they can be training and prepared to fight.

Belgium would be one of the countries to be hit because Germany would want to use that country as a gateway to France. Belgium has nothing to do with the problems but, they are just in the way.

The port at Brest was busy with food and military goods flooding the town. Those goods had to then be transferred to other allied countries and areas of Franch.

Jack and Piere were not old enough to fight and their parents wanted them to wait awhile to see if smarter people can prevent the war. If war came it would include France and both boys would be required to contribute. Young boys, like them, find war exciting, until they actually fight; then they find how dangerous it is. With other young boys, they were practicing with wooden guns and marching in order that they would have experience in what to do and how to behave as a real soldier.

Jack and Piere were not interested in going to war but, they knew that if war came, they would have to go. Their sister was still working at the hospital and she was getting good enough that she was permitted to do minor things like hand needles and bandage and other things to the nurse She liked the work and the men like to see here because she was so beautiful. She heard from the nurses that if the war came, they would go to several hospitals and with a shortage of doctors., they might have to operate so, the nurses were being trained on minor wound operations. Marie would be required to assist by handing the nurses the equipment. Most people would not like the work Marie was doing but she loved to contribute in any way she could.

CHAPTER 34

San Antonia, Texas 11/28/1908

Today was Thanksgiving Day and everybody wanted turkey. Since this was Texas, people would rather have brisket but for one day turkey with all the trimmings would do. Jason and Monica and their son George, were having a few neighbors over including an elderly couple who wanted to move to a retirement community in Florida but, they stayed to be close to the cemetery where their only son is buried. Their son Mark, fell in with a bad crowd and died of an over dose. His death devastated his parents and they decided to stay.

After a meal that lasted 2 hours, everyone was full from the large dinner and the kids went out to play and the adults spent time discussed the problems in Europe. They all agreed that we should stay out to protect our men from dying for Europe. They all agreed that if we are not attacked, stay home.

CHAPTER 35

Seaforth, England 8/14/1908

Arcie was old enough to be dating, and he is. Amanda was a pretty 16-year-old red head who fell into love with Archie. Neither one of them know anything about love but they both know that they have strong feelings for each other. They have gone for long walks to a park and had dinner with Archie's family and especially Archie's father could not be happier.

Amada lived two apartment houses from Archie and they saw a lot of each other through the years. Her family consisted of her parents and another sister, Bridget, who was two years older. They lived in a carbon copy apartment to Archie's and had a caring family with a father who worked at the port, and a mother who kept the apartment clean and makes wonderful meals.

Michael really likes Arcie but, it looks like Amanda has her hooks into him so Michael will have to settle for second base with Alexander. Alexander is tall and reassembly handsome so, he will do.

CHAPTER 36

Haskell County 1/5/1908

New years came in with a snow storm and Peter loved to play in the yard. and make a snowman. There was a long hill that most of the neighbor kids slide down with their sleds or toboggans. Peter loved to go down the hill all day. Usually, the hill is crowed because everyone wanted to slide even Sara went for a ride. Sam and Howard always followed Peter and Sara and they were fast becoming good friends. Peter just turned eight and he had to take care on the hill but, he always needed someone, like his mother or father to watch him. He is in fourth grade and with his fathers help he is doing so well that he could skip a grade but, he did not skip a grade now but, he will later.

It is amazing how fast eight years can pass; Jonathan and Rebecca look older than they are and they want to stop with the sick people in the office and they want to move to a warm place and spend their years relaxing with their son.

CHAPTER 37

━━ ❀ ━━

Braunau am Inn in Astria-Hungry 4/5/1908

Noah Wagner was born in the same town that Hitler was born in, Braunau am Inn in Austria-Hungry. It was possible that they may have met once or twice but Noah does not remember. Noah is 14 and still lives in the same small house with his father Otto and his mother Rachael. Otto is a plumber who works with two other plumbers in a small store where they keep their equipment. Noah is learning the trade so that he can work with his father when he finishes high school. Rachae; is a stay-at-home wife. Neither one is interested in politics but, you can't live where they live without getting involved with politics. There is no question that Noah will finish high school because people in this town know how important education is and no matter what field they enter they will be educated.

CHAPTER 38

San Antonio, Texas 5/1/1909

Today was special day because an air show was again coming to a large field outside of San Antonio. There were posters in every store to let people know when and where the show was taking place. George was so excited that he could not wait to go to the show. When Jason and Monica arrived at the field with their two-year old well-kept car there was hardly any space to park. The newly built grandstand was already full so they would have to stand to watch the show. The show consisted of two biplanes that were fitted with a special contraption that a man would hold on to while the pilot would make movements. This was known as wing walking and was dangerous. Because Juan and Leonard's family did not have a car, the boys came to the show with George. The show lasted 40 minutes after which you could pay $2 for a seven-minute ride. George and Leonard had saved their allowance money to take a ride. Juan decided to stay on the ground. The ride that George and Leonard took gave them a love for flying that they never lost and changed their life.

CHAPTER 39

———— ✹ ————

Brest Franch 8/12/1910

It is heating up in Brest and all over France and Europe. No body wants to talk and try to avoid war. Years of hatred have made it difficult to talk. Most counties have already ordered canons and new rifles and other weapons of war as well as food that can last. America is not sending goods to Germany and other countries that support Germany. America has plenty to sell but they are also selling to their own army and navy just in case. It seems that the whole world wants to fight. American factories were working overtime because the more goods they make especially military, the more money they make. They are making enough that they could sell to America if needed.

Jack and Marie notice that some of their neighbors have moved out to go to Spain. Spain is neutral and they and their families will be safe and not have to fight. Jack felt that if it comes to war, he wants to fight for his country so, he and his family are staying.

CHAPTER 40

— ❁ —

San Antonio, Texas 4/14/1910

Several cities, such as San Antonio hired a French teacher to teach the men likely to go to France basic French. Most men took the advantage of this opportunity to learn a new language even if they had to fight. The men hoped that they would not need to use the language because there would be no war, but knowing the language gives them a chance to "make friends "with the French woman. Some of the older boys would practice by speaking to each other in French and not English, which confused those that did not speak any French. It is the start of a new decade and every one is ten years older. So far things are quiet in Europe so everyone in America is happy they do not need to worry about war.

CHAPTER 41

San Antonio, Texas 4/14/1910

George was 10 and he has grown into a tall handsome boy who is driving girls crazy. He is too young to understand why but, for some reason Leonard seemed to want to be with him as much as the girls.

Spring is around the corner and George and his family are doing well. The measles seems to have bypassed most of the town and many residents. His family was spared so the father and mother were able to continue with their day-to-day activities. George was 10 now and he loved to ride his horse, Shorty, and play with his two best friends, Juan, and Leonard and the three of them went on as normal; school, riding, and playing America vs Germany games with BB's, until their parents stopped them. Guns, such as BB guns can still harm and in some cases kill. It the boys wanted to play; they needed wood guns. They may be playing war games but they have no idea how horrible and dangerous war can be and their parents did not want them to find out.

Leonard is showing more interest in George but George thought that he just wanted to be good friends, and he did but, not the way that he thinks. It would take another year before he knows what Leonard wants and George to quickly say "no."

CHAPTER 42

Haskell County 6/2/1909

The doctor's office was busy, as usual. If it wasn't measles, it was the flu; it was a miracle that the doctor and his family has been able to avoid what the patients were not able to avoid. Peter, did come down with a mild case of the measles but, with his father' care he was able to beat it.

At nine years old, Peter was doing well in school and his father would be sure to send him to a good college, hopefully to be a doctor.

Peter did not have many friends except for Sara, Sam, and Howard. For some reason the girls in school would talk when he passes them, and the talk seemed to be about him. They seemed to be jealous when they see him talking to Sara and he was too young to understand why. Boys progress later than girls when it comes to noticing the opposite sex. It would not be long before Peter will catch up and understand.

Sam and Howard, although of similar age, did not seem to get as much attention from the girls as Peter but, they will in a few years and matches and romances will be made.

CHAPTER 43

+—— ⊛ ——+

Seaforth, England 5/10/1910

Archie was 17 and Amanda was 18 and people were already talking about a wedding in a couple of years, and Andrew could not wait to see if Amada could give him a red headed granddaughter; of course, a possible war could change that.

Even though Archie was only 17 he felt that he did not want to wait any longer. He spoked to his father and Amanda's father to see what they thought about getting married. Both fathers agreed that another year is for the best so, Archie agreed to wait until next year, that will g them time to plan for the wedding, in the mean time Archie will buy an engagement ring.

The minimum age to fight is 18 so, next year Archie would be required to fight if there was a war. His brother was only 15 years old and two years behind him. Archie also completed the three-month program and he hated it and he hoped that the war would be over before he had to go.

CHAPTER 44

Brest Franch 8/12/1910

The town was busier than it's ever been. The workers worked longer hours at the port then then they ever have. Even young man such as, Jack and Piere worked at the port because there was work for them. They did not do the heavy lifting but they were able to do many of the smaller boxes, like food. In this way they are helping France in a small way.

Winter is coming on fast and that could delay the war because it is difficult on the troops to fight in the cold. People are also thinking about Christmas but they are doing a lot more praying by people on both sides to prevent the war.

Because it is obvious that if there will be a war, France would be involved, the French offices' have asked all males 18 and over to practice certain skills they might need if there was a war. Groups of men would practice marching and stick guns were used to practice with and other sticks were used to practice as knives.

CHAPTER 45

─── ✦ ───

Seaforth, England 7/10/1910

Mathew was 17 and did not have a girlfriend, which surprised a lot of people because he was so handsome. He was not gay he just did not find anyone who he felt comfortable with. His mother could not work as many hours any more because she was getting sick all the time. Mathew will finish high school next year and he will get a job to help pay the bills so his mother will not need to work as much anymore. Mary had to spend money to see a doctor to see why she was week and sick all the time. The doctor did not need long to know what was Mary's problem; the flu. The flu is going around and is very easy to catch; you can catch it by physical contact or from a cough and it can be deadly but in Mary's case she survived, but not the next time.

This strain of the flu was not as bad as other strains to come but, it was still bad enough to kill people. This" Spanish Flu" was spreading all over the world and it was very viral. In 1910 it was not as strong as it would get in 1918-1920. When Mary caught the flu for the second time, she could not survive. The family was not as affected but they did mourn her because she was a wonderful wife and mother.

CHAPTER 46

Braunau am Inn in Austria-Hungry 6/30/1910

So far early summer has been rainy, almost every day has seen some amount of rain. The work load was heavy as usual, and Noah was learning to be a good and careful plumber. His father is happy how his son was turning out; good grades in school; he will graduate next year and, a good worker; all he needs now is to find a wife. He had been friends for years with some girls but for some reason they did not seem to hit It off; they were more like brother and sister then boyfriend and girlfriend. There was no excuse for the lack of a romantic relation, it was just one of those things.

A young woman, Nora the same age as Noah, noticed him and he finally noticed a woman. She was as tall as him and for some reason she smelled nice. She wanted to be a teacher but, she liked to paint and that is what Noah smelled, as well as love.

Noah was set with a good future and Nora was the artist type, painting, and sculpturing. It had nothing to do with money, she just liked to paint; you can always find her in a park when the weather was good with people watching her and wanting to buy a picture in the hope, she becomes famous and the picture would be worth money. Her painting takes her mind and the watchers mind off politics so it was good theapy for all.

Although she liked to paint, she liked children more, and she wanted a job teaching; that will for sure, bring in some money from a salary.

CHAPTER 47

———— ✾ ————

Haskell County 6/10/1912

Peter was 12 years old and Sara and Peter had been close since they were three. They were too young to be in love and for Peter to go to a tent city to train. They were both in different classes but they did walk home together. The doctor was busy as usual, with flu patients; more than usual. It is the end of Fall but people were still getting sick. Peter wore a homemade mask and that did such a good job that other people made their own mask. So many people were wearing masks that it looked like a giant masquerade party.

The news in Europe was bleak and people were guessing when the war will start. With the good weather, the war could start any day.

The measles epidemic is still raging and many people in the region have been mutilated by the bumps, some lost eye sight with measles on the face, and many have died. Several good friends of the doctor have died and the worse is yet to come.

CHAPTER 48

San Antonia, Texas 4/14/1912

George was 12 and he could really ride his horse, Shorty, No one his age could ride as fast or as well as George. He was very popular with the girls and with Leonard but, George was getting bothered by Leonard, he wished that he would bother someone else. George does not know much about girls but he knows that he likes them and not boys.

School was almost over for the season and then Jason can relax. George is almost old enough and good enough that he could easily win some money in races. Shorty is getting older but, George takes good care of him.

Savana, named after her father's birthplace, is a school mate of George and is at an age, 12 and she notices him and he notices her. She is one of those girls who develops early with large breasts that make her, what is called, a "looker." Adding her blond hair and all the boys notice her, but she only notices George.

CHAPTER 49

─── ❀ ───

Brest Franch 11/12/1912

Winter was almost here and it is not likely that the war would start now. The piers are busy no matter the weather. Every day there is more bad news regarding the possibility of war. Germany is getting more and more loud with Serbia and each side has allies. As usual, America is staying out of the problems; but they are still training the men in case they need to go to war.

Father John has asked his superier, the bishop, for additional oil and other supplies that would be used to treat the wounded, and to give last rights. A retired priest is available to handle the parish but, with his age it will be a problem. Father John may need to split his time between the parish and the war. Nobody said it was easy being a priest.

CHAPTER 50

＊＝ ── ❀ ── ＝＊

Seaforth, England 10/10/1912

Winter was here and it may be too early for Christmas but, the two boys are still thinking about gifts, even at their age. This year Archie was going to give Amanda a ring, the best that he can afford. He really did love her and he knows that she loves him. Both families are wishing that there is no war because Archie and Amanda make such a nice couple.

The families have started to make plans for a small wedding while Archie and Amanda have found a clean, small apartment, just the right size for them to start life together and start a family. Archie will work at the dock to support his family, while Amanda will find local work until she becomes a mother.

CHAPTER 51

Briest, Franch 3/08/1913

Jack was now 20 and for sure be expected to fight in the expected war. His brother Piere was younger but, still expected to fight. Their parents were terrified about what could happen to them. The reports claim that if there was a war, thousands of men are expected to die daily from both sides. Everyone wants America to help, but America did not want to enter the coming blood bath. Their parents did not like the idea of both brothers fighting, especially how bloody the battles are expected to be. At least Piere was 18 and finished his training and was prepared to fight if necessary.

Marie was just 14 and was so beautiful that every male in town drooled over her even though she was so young. There was no doubt that she would need to stay in the house for her own perfection. She had started more extensive work with the nurses. She could go things like bandage wounds and clean waste units. She will be a big help in the war

CHAPTER 52

Seaforth, England 2/10/1913

The date has arrived and the wedding has taken place. A local minister will say the prays to marry them. He knew them both for most of their lives and he thought that they make a wonderful couple. The families knew each other, they both loved each other, Archie had a good job and Amanda was studding to be a nurse. It could not be a better match.

Both families have chipped in for an intimate wedding with just the close family attending. Their apartment came furnished so they did not need to spend money for any furniture, but with luck they will need to buy things for a baby.

The rules to serve in the army allowed a family with a new baby to let the male to stay home for one year to help care for his wife and child. In addition, if there are two or more young children the male would be exempt from active duty. With luck, Amanda will have a child soon, before Archie needs to go to war.

Alexander loved Amanda just as much as Archie but she loved Archie. Even though Archie was his brother it bothered him to lose Amanda. Alexanda was dating him and she was ok and would make a fine wife, but he was still jealous of Archie.

CHAPTER 53

Haskell, County 6/27,1914

Things were very hot in Europe and every county had bought as much military equipment as possible. If there is a war it is going to be a blood bath because of all the countries fighting. America was very strongly antiwar and the only things that they would support would be sending food and equipment to the allies. Peter was only 14 years old and he would be safe at home even if there was a war and that is how his parents like it. Some of the neighbors are thinking of a way to keep their sons from enlisting or volunteering. Peter did think about volunteering for the French air force but, he had to wait for a few more years. He thought about taking lessons from someone that sells planes but, there is no way that his parents would let him fly a plane that is falling apart so he would have to wait a couple more years to go to Franch.

CHAPTER 54

San Antonio, Texas 6/27/1914

It is a nice day in San Antonio. After 3 straight days of rain, the sun is finally shining and there is only a slight warm wind, which made it a perfect day. People are smiling and happy to be alive. A rodeo was in town and no native Texan would miss that. George was getting to be a fine rider with his horse, Shorty, he could out race any of the other kids in the neighbor. He does not know what he wants to do when he grows up, but he will still ride for fun.

The word from Europe was that there is going to be a war and it is coming any day now. There is a rumor that there may be an assentation and depending on who it was, and who did the assignation could be the match that started a fire that no one could put out,

America fought a recent war with Mexico and that was another reason that people were not interested in another war so, it was pretty sure that they would not go to war "over there."

CHAPTER 55

Brest Franch 6/27/1914

The port was the busiest it has ever been. People have been working a double shift in order to empty the ships and load the train cars to go to the final destination. Every one who is capable of the work is working. Jack is 21 and Piere is 19, and both can work and be called to fight. Even the young girls, such as Pat, did what they could to help, even if they did not get paid.

Marie was 14 and had started to train at the hospital to work with the nurses. Every one who was a male and could breath noticed Marie but with her age all they would do was say "hi". In a few years they will say more and she will be able to work as a nurse by herself.

Father John had a special mass to pray for peace and many people went because the people wanted peace and they believed that praying together was a good way to talk to God. Father John received permission from his bishop that if there was a war that he would accompany the troops and pray with them and pray over the wounded and the dead.

CHAPTER 56

Braunau am Inn in Austria-Hungry 6/27/1914

It was a sunny, warm day and Noah and his father were busy as usual. There was a large pipe install project that will require the entire team. Noah had finally met a young girl and he had a first date with her. Her name was Megan, not exactly a Germany name, but a name that her mother liked. She was tall and blonde, like many German girls. For some reason Noah fell for her and she fell for him. It could be worse, he had a good job and that made him prime husband material so her parents were happy, especially since he was not a Jew.

Now that he is older, Noah is concerned with the possibility of a war. He was old enough that he had to fight after a brief training period. Because he was in a important profession he did not have to go to a sort of base camp but, he cannot avoid that now if there was a war. Just when he finally met a girl, he might lose her to war.

CHAPTER 57

Seaforth, England 6/27/1914

It was a nice day and a perfect day to work; it was warm but not hot like a July day, a light wind and perfect for working. The port was open and workers were hard at work. Archie and Alexander work at the pier just like their father has for years.

Things are getting worse with the anger that people are showing to each other. Even in America, with it's large German population non-German people are starting to avoid the Germans and refuse to talk to them because they felt that the Germans may be the cause of a war.

People are betting on which day the war will start. Whoever picked tomorrow, will win.

CHAPTER 58

Seaforth, England 6/27/1914

Like most of his friends, Mathew had finished his three months of training so in case there is a war he would have some basic training. His mother was getting sick all the time and she could not bear to see her only child training for war. He was working at the pier, just like his father and he does not have someone to live his life with. It was curious that none of the eligible girls were interested in Mathew, but they were; They just were waiting for him to ask someone out. Working at the pier was giving him large muscles that were notable to the girls and made him more desirable. Maybe tomorrow he will ask someone out.

Bridget noticed and so did other girls. Bridget was a medium sized blonde girl that to most men would be considered beautiful especially since she was big in front for her age. But Mathew did notice and he was going to ask her out tomorrow. But things changed that.

PART 2

War

CHAPTER 1

War in Europe 6/28/1914

One shot is all it took to light the fuse.

Growing tension between countries in Europe came to a head on June,28,1914 when a Bosnian Serbia named Gavrilo Princip accessioned Archduke Franz Ferdinand heir to the Austro-Hungarian throne. This caused two sides in the battle to be created: Serbia, Russia, France, and United Kingdom, together known as The Triple Entente, later to join was Japan, Italy, and America. On the other side the Central Powers consisting of German Empire, Austria-Hungary, the Ottoman Empire, and Bulgaria.

Other countries, such as Belgium were involved because fighting took place there. England and France wanted and later were desperate for America to join. But America was not interested in a foreign war.

CHAPTER 2

＊＊＊＊ — ✸ — ＊＊＊＊

Training Outside Brest 7/2/1914

It did not take long for the fighting to start and as a result trading in France was done as quickly as possible. No one knew how the battles would be fought so the training was with rifles and bayonets. As things started getting more and more likely for war, many countries started training before the fatal shot occurred. Franch was one of those countries.

Jack and Piere had started training two months before the war started. Jack was going to be in the infantry while Piere was going to volunteer for the French air force. He wanted to learn to fly. Of course, their parents, like most parents were terrified of what could happen to them but, they had no choice, all able body male, 18 and over had to train. Now they see how important that early training was, they are ready for the real training at the base. The base that they went to was a tent camp where each tent could each hold 30 soldiers which helped spread colds, measles, and the flu. Each tent had a stove that could barely keep the people inside warm. Although they did not know what the conditions were on the other side, they were probably similar.

Marie was working hard to become a fully educated nurse who can help with the wounded. The soldiers must think that they went to heaven when they see the angel, Marie. She is working hard but, at 15 she can not be permitted to go to a field hospital but, she can stay where she is at the local hospital and continue her education there.

CHAPTER 3

Seaforth, England 6/28/1914

The shot that started the war was not loud but it caused trouble around the world. The news about the shot and the start of the war, did not take long to reach England and for England to support France a country that will be sure to be attacked and news hit the wires almost as if the radio was waiting for the news. The war that no one wants has started. With the three-month training program, UK soldiers, from all parts of the kingdom, such as Canada, India, and other places will be called into action.

The war that most people prayed would not come has come, and it will affect almost every family in England in one way or another. The Wallace family has two sons that are trained to fight. Both Archai and Alexander completed their three-month training requirement period, that will not be anything like the real thing, but they will fight for their country.

CHAPTER 4

San Antonio, Texas 6/29/1914

The news about the war hit the papers the next day. The news was not just in large print but took the entire front page just one word "WAR". The army bases started gearing up for the expected group of men who wanted experience and adventure; so far there was no need for enlistment. There were very little real weapons because with no wars to fight, there was no need for supplies; however; the army is gearing up to train with real weapons. The recruits used wooden guns to learn how to hold a gun and to shot and march. Since this was Texas, most of the recruits already knew how to shot since they were over 18 and still had their own rifles to train with. They did not know that they would need to practice how to dig trenches, that would come later for real.

People did not believe that America would go to war because no one wanted to go and because the president said that "He kept us out of war." It would take an attack from Germany to cause America to declare war. No country is that stupid.

George, along with his three friends, Juan and Leonard, and Mathew were too young to train or fight but they still went to the small training center to watch other people who were old enough to learn how to be soldiers. They had backpacks to learn how to pack as well as other things to learn that could keep them alive. They wanted to learn but their parents wanted them to stay home.

CHAPTER 5

Haskell, County 6/29/1914

Even in a small county like Haskell, the news of war warranted large font for the front page. Nobody was talking about any thing else except the war and if America would be forced to fight as well. Some counties, like Haskell, asked able bodied men of age, to go to the fairground to practice marching, how to salute and other things that they would need to learn. Peter was only 14 but he and others too young to fight went to see others train. At their age they were excited but their parents were afraid. The one thought on the adult mind's was that the president better keep his promise to stay out of the war.

Sara, Peter's friend, was concerned about Peter getting hurt if he went to war because she had puppy love over him. Sara wanted to be a newspaper writer when she grows up and that might require her going to France to report the war and that might put her in as much danger as a solider. She, like most people in town, hoped that the war would be over fast.

CHAPTER 6

Brest, Franch 7/30/1914

Marie turned into a beautiful young woman and she was just 15 years old. She was being examined by the men in Brest and soldiers whenever she left the house. Her father restricted her to the house as much as possible and he wanted her brothers to watch her when she goes out but, they were at camp learning to use the equipment that would kill the enemy. He was concerned what would happen to her if the war hit Brest and what the soldiers would do to her.

She knew some friends who were nurses and were expected to help with the wounded and she wanted to help so she went to the hospital and worked as an aide which allowed her to do minor work but, also to get used to procedures. Of course, her father did not want her to do that kind of work but, he was proud that she wanted to help.

The boys, Jack and Piere were old enough to fight but like most people they did not want to fight, but both of them had to train because all eligible men needed to support their country. It was during this training that the doctors discovered that Piere was unfit to serve because he had damaged his right shoulder working at the dock. Piere was not happy that he could not help but his parents were glad that one son would be safe.

CHAPTER 7

Braunau am Inn in Austria-Hungry 11/27/1914

Noah was old enough to serve even with his work exemption. He had not had the original training because of the work exemption but now he is training hard to catch up to the recruits that already were trained. Nora was very upset because Noah had proposed and the wedding date was set up for three weeks from now and that had to be cancelled.

So far Germany was doing well, French was already in trouble, and the war may quickly be over, as long as America stayed out of the war. Germany knew that America did not want to enter the war so they were doing there best to be peaceful to them and not make any trouble. They knew that there were a large number of German people living in the midwest and they for sure did not wany to go to war with the father land, so for this time America was not in the picture.

CHAPTER 8

—— ❋ ——

First Battle of Ypres: October 19 to November 22, 1914

One of the first major battles of the war was the First Battle of Ypres. The first of three battles to control the ancient Flemish city on Belgium's north coast that allows access to the English Channel ports and the North Sea. The massive conflict involving an estimated 600,000 Germans and 420,000 Allies—continues for three weeks until brutal winter weather brings it to an end. typical of so many World War I battles, both sides engage in trench warfare and suffered massive casualties, but neither could claim a victory. With the kind of losses suffered by both sides this will be the bloodiest war in history. Although Germany had more soldiers killed, after you add all the allies killed, Britan, France, and Belgium the total came close.

Jack suffered two wounds from scrapple but the wounds were not serious but, he was transferred to a field hospital to be patched up. With the brutal winter weather, it was not possible to fight so, Jack went to a nearby tent camp to rest and fill his backpack with supplies. Because of his service he received a medal and a promotion. There was hot food available but only a few stoves for the tents to keep warm and with the coming of mid-winter all you could do was stay as warm as you could.

Piere did not pass the physical because he had a bad arm that he damaged at the docks. He did help by doing paper work at the base but, he never lost his love for flying.

Even though Marie was only 15 she was able to help at the local hospital and is learning enough that if the war does not end soon, she will be able to work at one of the field hospitals. Her father was so proud of his family.

CHAPTER 9

Christmas Truce 1914

The Christmas truce was a series of widespread unofficial ceasefires along the Western Front of the First World War around Christmas 1914.

The truce occurred five months after hostilities had begun. Lulls occurred in the fighting as armies ran out of men and munitions and commanders reconsidered their strategies following the stalemate of the Race to the Sea and the indecisive result of the First Battle of Ypres. In the week leading up to Christmas, French, German and British soldiers crossed trenches to exchange seasonal greetings and talk. In some areas, men from both sides ventured into no man's land on Christmas Eve and Christmas Day to mingle and exchange food and souvenirs. There were joint burial ceremonies and prisoner swaps, while several meetings ended in singing. Hostilities continued in some sectors, while in others the sides settled on little more than arrangements to recover bodies.

The following year, a few units arranged ceasefires but the truces were not nearly as widespread as in 1914; this was, in part, due to strongly worded orders from commanders, prohibiting truces. Soldiers were no longer amenable to truce increasingly bitter after the human losses suffered during the battles of 1915

CHAPTER 10

Haskell, County 9/28/1914

It was fall but it already felt like winter. Dr. Guest and his wife, Rebecca, along with their son Peter were over whelmed with patients with the flu. Like the measles epidemic there was not enough room for patients in the office or even in the nearby hospital. Some people were so desperate for help that that they kidnaped nurses to take care of their families. So many people were dying t and there was no place to store the bodies. There were no coffins for the bodies and families had to dig their own graves. Priests and police would remove bodies. People would put bodies outside and an open truck or wagon would come by to pick them up.

No one could look at the trucks or wagons that carried the bodies. The bodies were wrapped in cloth and stacked loosely on other bodies wrapped in cloth, arms and legs protruding, bodies heading for cemeteries to be buried in trenches – or hear the mourners and the call for the dead, and not think of another plague – the plague of the Middle Ages.

CHAPTER 11

Hitler in World War 1

Hitler fought in several battles during World War 1. One battle was the Battle of Somme and the other was the First Battle of Ypres; both in an infantry division. He was wounded by shrapnel in one, and blinded by a mustard gas attack, and had his life spared by a decorated British officer. In the battle when his life was saved, Hitler was retreating from a battle and turned around to see where the British soldiers were when the officer pointed the rifle at him but did not fire at the retreating soldier. The result of that non shooting resulted in good part, the cause of World War 2 and the death of between 70 and 85 million people, including both military personnel and civilians. One shot caused World War 1 and the lack of a shot caused World War 2.

CHAPTER 12

San Antonio, Texas 11/29/1914

It did not take long for France to ask America to send troops to help but, America did not have people trained and America was not at war. The battles were becoming more forceful and bloodier with thousands of men killed and wounded. With more powerful, weapons, such as mustard gas and tanks to come the numbers will rise but, America will stay firm about not sending untrained troops to fight.

George, like most fourteen-year-old boys, was excited about the war and so were his friends Juan and Leonard, but, they did not want o go to war. The three of them went to a shooting range and practiced with their BB guns and 22's. They also watched the recruits march, shot, and do other things that one day they might have to do for real and killing a person is harder than shooting a target. It was fun to watch but not to the parents of these young boys.

CHAPTER 13

One of the First Major Battles – Battle of the Mons 8/22/1914

One of the first major battles, the Battle of Mons 8/22/1914, takes place in Mons, Belgium, with a British Expeditionary Force that numbers about 75,000 fighting an estimated 150,000 Germans in an attempt to hold the Mons-Conde Canal. In the final of four "Battles of the Frontier" held in the first weeks of World War I, the British forces were overpowered and forced to retreat, handing the Germans a strategic victory. Some 1,600 British and 5,000 Germans casualties are reported. One of the wounded was Archie. He had nowhere to hide because the trench was not built yet. He was fortunate that he was taken to a camp hospital to recover. The battle earned him a medal but, he had to go back to fight. Father John tended to many wounded and dying British soldiers and he, himself was wounded but he was sent to a camp hospital to be patched up and was sent back to a hospital to, recover from multiple wounds. While in the hospital he tended to the wounded. He went into the heart of the battle to give numerous soldiers the last rites. Many soldiers from both sides and the Germans let him pray over soldiers from both sides. It was more and more obvious that France and Britan needed the Americans, and soon, or the war would be over soon. Germany has many more troops and weapons to fight with. Even if they lost more men in a battle they still had more to spare.

CHAPTER 14

—✦— ❂ —✦—

Battle of Tannenberg 8/1914

Dubbed the Battle of Tannenberg by the victorious Germans, this would be the country's biggest win against Russia along the Eastern Front. This was the first battle that Noah was in and he did a good job considering only a week's training. He did such a good job attacking Russian soldiers that he was promoted and given a medal to brag about. The battle begins with Russian armies attacking German troops in German East Prussia (now Poland) from the south and the east, which, at first, works. But, after intercepting unencripted radio messages from the Russians, the Germans are able to reorganize their strategy, forcing the Russians into retreat. The Germans pursued the Russians, essentially annihilating the armies with 30,000 casualties and more than 90,000 taken prisoner. This battle was devastating for the allies and gave the Germans a boost to their moral and made the Russians more ready to give up.

CHAPTER 15

Haskell, County 10/28/1914

The only way that people could get their news was with the paper or the radio and news about the war is nonstop. Every day the news is usually about the thousands of soldiers killed. The new weapon called a plane was used to bomb from the air. France had a volunteer air force that many Americans were volunteering for. Most Americans did not volunteer for battle of any kind because all the reports say that the allies were being killed by the thousands and no one volunteers for that unless, they have friends or relatives In France or England and they wanted to help them in one way or another

The planes flown were flimsy, and not as safe as those of later years. Engines and other parts failed, and machine-guns often jammed when they were needed. The planes could crash without being shot at. One man asked to be moved back to his infantry unit, where "he could be safe."

CHAPTER 16

San Antonio, Texas 2/30/1915

George was now 15 and getting closer to being called to battle training but, fortunately, America was not at war. The only Americans fighting in the war were those who volunteered to fight on the ground from trenches, or from the air and risk getting shot down. The battles were very bloody because so many men were involved. Later battles were even worse because mustard gas was involved. If you were not killed by suffocation from the gas but just wounded, you were horribly disfigured. Hitler was affected by the gas because he had a large mustache and his gas mask could not fit, that caused him to trim his mustache to a small size so the mask could fit next time. That is the mustache that he is known for.

George was very popular with the young girls and with Leonard. One girl, Savana, named after her father's birthplace, in particular, wanted to date George but George did not seem interested in anyone at this time. Savana was very pretty and other boys noticed her but she still wanted George. It is obvious that Leonard may be more interested in boys like George then the girls; is it possible that George is the same. It was time for Savana to take the bull by the horns and ask George for a date. That is not proper for a girl to do in Texas in 1915 but she asked any way. So, Savana went up to George when he was alone, which he seldom is, and asked him if would like to meet after school and work on the math homework together. Unknown to Savana, George was interested in her but, he was too shy to ask, now he was glad that she asked first. And so, a romance began.

CHAPTER 17

———— ❁ ————

Brest, Franch 7/30/1914

France and Belgium were getting the worse of the battles, with thousands of their troops being killed or wounded at every battle. The war had just started and people are saying "Where are the Americas." They were working in tent camps just in case but, they can not wait much more, because the way it looks the war will be over before the Americans can get to France.

Americans still believe that this is a "Foreign War" and they should protect their sons, husbands, and daughters from fighting. Just in case, there were many tent camps being set up for troops to practice what men might have to do. All mem from 18 to 30 must train for three months to prepare to fight. Now that they know they may have to fight in trenches they are digging the trenches and learning what that is about. They also practice how to live in one. America is getting ready but they need a reason to go to war.

CHAPTER 18

— ⊛ —

Haskell, County 12/10/1915

There would be no big Christmas celebration this year because no one was in a mode to celebrate. Most families had at least one young man in the family practicing at a made-up camp. Now that they know what to expect if America enters the war, they knew what to practice. Because it was winter and one of the coldest winters, they will wait for the sprint to practice with a rifle and marching and how to dig and live in a trench.

Sara and Peter were becoming more friendly and if there was no war they would probably get married. Sara had made it to finish eighth grade, which was impressive for a girl in those days. Peter is in senior class in high school and heading for college in the hope of becoming a doctor like his father, who is proud of his son.

Life at home was not easy for Peter's parents. They are old for those times, they were always around sick people, and it's winter when lots of older people die from colds and pneumonia. Peter does not want to lose them because they loved him and they took care of him better than any one else could and most of all, because he loves them.

CHAPTER 19

━━ ✦ ━━

Battle of Verdun: February 21
to December 18, 1916

The battle of Verdun becomes World War 1's longest single battle that lasts nearly a year as the French Army fends off a surprise German offensive that causes mass losses on both sides, with more than 600,000 total casualties. Jack was wounded again and was driven to a camp hospital to be recover and be sent back to fight. French soldiers were dying by the thousands and a wounded soldier, unless he lost a limb had to go back to fight.

In an attempt to cripple France's part in the war and cause a massive blow to its army's morale, the Germans choose to attack the fort of Verdun, France's part in the war and cause a massive blow to its army's morale, the Germans choose to attack the fort of Verdun, begin retaking the stronghold and, as winter sets in and during the first Battle of the Somme rages, the Verdun fighting finally comes to an end.

During this battle Father John prayed over and gave last rights to hundreds of French soldiers. During this time, he was wounded twice but went back to serve the French and Germans. He wore a hat with a cross on it for soldiers to see but, he was wounded for the third and final time as he was giving last rights to a young French private. Two other French soldiers risked their lives to drag the father back to have his body sent back to his parish.

For Father John's heroism he received the Volunteer Combatant's Cross and the Croix de guerre 1914–1918 from France and the Life Saving medal from Germany. He was the only person to be awarded from both sides.

CHAPTER 20

Brest, Franch 6/30/1916

There were very few caskets of any quality available but, the people in the town found one for Father John. The entire parish came out for his memorial mass. The bishop was also there to say the mass, a big honor for a priest. The medals were posted on his flock and he was buried on the church grounds. He will be missed from the parish and from the field of battle. A picture of him and another of his medals hung in the church so people can remember him and his bravery. Many people think he is a saint and pray to him and the church has started proceedings to investigate his right to be called a saint. Becoming a saint takes a long time. It requires two miracles attributed to the person, examine the person's life and other things and it takes years. In Father John's case the process was still taking place even after the war was over.

CHAPTER 21

Battle of the Somme July to November 1916

The Battle of the Somme, which took place from July to November 1916, began as an Allied offensive against German forces along the Western Front of World War 1, near the Somme River in France. The battle turned into one of the most bitter, deadly, and costly battles in all of human history, as British forces suffered more than 57,000 casualties—including more than 19,000 soldiers killed—on the first day of the battle alone. Noah acted bravely and received two more medals for his bravely and he received two more medals when he was killed at Gallipoli. By the time the Battle of the Somme (sometimes called the First Battle of the Somme) ended nearly five months later, more than 3 million soldiers on both sides had fought in the battle, and more than 1 million had been killed or wounded.

Noah's parents did not hear about him being wounded but, they did about him being killed at Gallipoli, and they were crushed. They knew that it could happen but, they were not expecting it. Nora cried for days until she was empty of tears. She never recovered from Noah's death.

The age has been changed for those British citizens to serve from 17 to 45 years old. This meant more older soldiers getting killed and wounded. Both Alexander and his father Andrew were wounded in the early stage of this battle. Both were patched up and driven to a field hospital for more treatment. In the field hospital they were treated by a young beautiful French nurse aid, called Marie, that all the wounded wanted to be treated by. Andrew had more serious wounds but he survived and was sent home. His son recovered and went to battle again; where he was wounded and killed at Gallipoli.

CHAPTER 22

The Battle of Gallipoli 2/15 1/16

The Battle of Gallipoli, also known as the Gallipoli Campaign, was a battle of World War I that was fought on the Gallipoli peninsula. It was fought between February 1915 and January 1916. Britain and France, who were Russia's allies, intended to secure the peninsula from the Ottoman Empire. They launched an attack on the peninsula with the sole objective of capturing Constantinople, which is the modern Istanbul, and was the Ottoman capital. The campaign was abandoned after several months of fighting with thousands of causalities on both sides, including Mathew, and the invasion forces retreated to Egypt. The Battle of Gallipoli was a major victory for the Ottomans and is considered as a defining moment in the history of Turkey. It formed the background on which the Turkish War of Independence was fought.

CHAPTER 23

Seaforth, England 4/28/1916

The notice struck Mathew's family hard, even though they knew that with the casualty rate it was possible that Mathew could be wounded or killed. The notice did not come, to Bridget herself but Mathew' father, who knew of their friendship and told her. Although Mathew and Bridget never made plans to be married, they felt it would happen if they survived the war. With a stiff upper lip of the British, she was able to remain calm even though she was mad at the loss of life. She was able to, with time, to sail to America and find someone to help her forget.

CHAPTER 24

━━━━ ❁ ━━━━

French Army Mutinies 1917

The 1917 French Army mutinies took place amongst French Army troops on the Western Front in Northern Franch. They started just after the unsuccessful and costly Second Battle of the Aisne. The new French commander of the armies in France, General Robert Nivelle had promised a decisive victory over the Germans in 48 hours; morale in French armies rose to a great height and the shock of failure soured their mood overnight.

The mutinies and associated disruptions involved, to various degrees, nearly half of the French infantry divisions stationed on the Western Front. The term "mutiny" does not precisely describe events; soldiers remained in trenches and were willing to defend but refused orders to attack. Nivelle was sacked and replaced by General Philippe Petain, who restored morale by talking to the men, promising no more suicidal attacks, providing rest and leave for exhausted units and moderating discipline. He held 3,400 court martials in which 554 mutineers were sentenced to death and 26 were executed.

Jack was not in one of the units that had refused to fight so he was not disciplined, the fact that he had fought in battles before, received medals, and was promoted, made him untouched.

The news about the sinking of an American ship and then four more brings the Allies to a state of joy because they know that America will declare war and be coming to help and none too soon. The youth of their countries are being slathered and they need America to help. Germany made a major mistake because they were on their way to beating France and England but, now, the tide will turn.

PART 3

America Enters the War

CHAPTER 1

＋—————— ✸ ——————＋

The Russian Revolution 1914

Germany was fighting on two fronts, the east and the west front. Like Napolean before and Hitler later, and Germany is learning now, you do not fight Russia in winter.

Russia entered World War 1 in August 1914 in support of the Serbs and their French and British allies. Their involvement in the war would soon prove disastrous for the Russian Empire. Russia was still recovering from a losing war with Japan and could not afford to enter another war. The population was improvised and did not need another war and were primed for a revolution. Even though Rusia was weak they still had a large army that had experience in fighting. The Russian army was tired from the last war and were ready to surrender and they just needed a push and Germany gave the push. They helped Lenin get to Russia and start a revolution that cased Russia to surrender. This surrender caused one front to collapse and helped Germany that now had more troops to fight France and their allies. If America stayed out, they would win. Once they entered, it was a new ball game.

CHAPTER 2

America into War

The nation was against entering the "Foreign war." People could not see why American men and women should risk their lives for others. President Wilson ran on a platform of "He kept us out of war." With Britan and France losing thousands of soldiers every day, they were desperate for America to enter the war. One reason that America was not interested in going to war was because of the large number of Germans living in America. It was possible that without a good reason to enter, they might riot. Then two things happened that gave them the reason.

Widespread protest over the sinking by U-boat of the British ocean liner Lusitania traveling from New York to Liverpool, England with hundreds of American passengers onboard—in May 1915 helped turn the tide of American public opinion against Germany. In February 1917, Congress passed a $250 million arms appropriations bill intended to make the United States ready for war.

Germany sunk four more U.S. merchant ships the following month, and on April 2 Woodrow Wilson appeared before Congress and called for a declaration of war against Germany.

The Zimmermann Telegram was a secret diplomatic communication issued from the German Foreign Office in January 1917 that proposed a military contract between the German Empire and Mexico if the United States entered World War I against Germany. With Germany's aid, Mexico would recover Texas, Arizona, and New Mexico. The telegram was intercepted by British intelligence.

Revelation of the contents enraged Americans, especially after German State Secretary for Foreign Affairs Arthur Zimmermann publicly admitted on March 3, 1917, that the telegram was genuine. It helped to generate support for the American declaration of war.

CHAPTER 3

America getting ready for War

Also known as “Black Jack,” John J. Pershing was a United States Army officer, serving in World War I as the commander of the American Expeditionary Forces {AEF| and he would oversee all American troops in the war.

He was notable for refusing to have his American soldiers integrated into British and French forces, as well as allowing all-black units to fight within the French army One of the big issues that he had was the fierce request by the French and British military leaders to get the American troops in the battle now. He knew that they were not ready to fight because they had limited training at home. They needed more training before they could fight. Another issue was that they wanted American troops to be under control of French and British offices, which he refused. He was not popular with the French and British leaders but he held strong.

CHAPTER 4

—✦— ❀ —✦—

Fort Sill

Men were lining up to enlist in the army. Weapons that were to be sent overseas were now diverted for Americas troops. Camps were being prepared for the new recruits and people who had served in previous military action were coming back to help train the new recruits. One such person was Lieutenant Harry S. Truman. He enlisted in the Missouri National Guard from 1905 and served until 1911. After America went to war, Harry went to a tent city at Fort Sill, Oklahoma for more training. After he went into battle and proved what he could do, he was promoted to Captain. With him in Fort Sill were thousands of recruits such as Juan Ortiz, who entered as a sergeant. He was made a sergeant because he was one of the few who graduated high school and he could drive a car. Truman would learn about the latest artillery along with those recruits, such as Juan who wanted to go into artillery and fire a "big" gun.

Fort Sill had an artillery range where men could learn how and when to use each weapon.

Artillery was the primary weapon of land warfare in World War I. Artillery was the principal threat to ground troops in the war and was the main reason for the development of trench warfare.

Artillery is generally split into two categories: light artillery and heavy artillery. Light artillery, commonly known as field artillery, is designed to be light enough and easy to transport on the battlefield. The need for light weight limited the size of the shells and the damage they could inflict on the enemy.

Another way to category is: guns, howitzer, and mortar. All three were there so the troops could learn how and when to use, each weapon.

George had no choice, he was assigned to the army as a corporal, who had hope to become a sergeant; the stripes on his sleeve would look good and may help to meet French women.

Leonard was barely eligible to fight but he wanted to go to Europe to learn how to fly. Some of his friends like Juan was not in a hurry to go but if called he would go to Europe. Other friends like George were in between, not in a hurry but will go if called. Those people who were in a hurry to go to fight soon found out how war really is. It is dirty, cold, dangerous and the food is awful.

Camp lasted for two months, which was not enough for the troops to be ready to fight. They will get more training at French camps even though the French want them to start fighting when they hit the ground. Pershing will not give up on the demands of the French and British general, because he deemed it too dangerous and he won.

CHAPTER 5

Train from Fort Sill to New York

After the two months training at Fort Sill, the troops were ready to take a train to their next destination. After saying good bye to people at the station who were crying because they did not know if they would every see them again, and many would not. The troops boarded the train, some also crying, for their trip to New York where they would board a ship to France, and the French were ecstatic that the Americans were finally coming.

The train from Fort Sill was packed with troops who were beginning to smell and stink up the train because they were packed so tight and some were making animal noise when the farted. No telling what the crowed troop ship will be like.

George had left the train with thousands of other troops. The Great War still seemed far away and he was worried that it would be over before he could get there. The French and English had been fighting for years already and he did not want to miss the fun. George was too young to understand what he is getting into, and it was not fun.

CHAPTER 6

Ship to France

The next part of the troop's journey was the ship George Washington, It was a large ship with a full cargo of troops. One soldier on board was an officer, Harry Truman. Truman had experience in the army but not in a troop ship and, it was an experience. Everyone on board was worried about the Germans sinking the ship. Now that they are at war state, that would be legal.

The ship was more crowed than the train and people were getting sea sick and caching the flu because it is easy to spread. There are a lot of people on top so they can get some fresh air and so they can vomit over the railing instead of inside. Hopefully once they land at a place called Brest, France it should be better.

CHAPTER 7

—✦— ❁ —✦—

New York to Brest, France

The George Washington docked, along with another troop ship from New York. The sun was shining so they knew it was around 1pm. The troops were happy to get off and line up for muster. As usual Marie, as well as many other girls checked out the new Americans and wonder how many will make it home. The French troops are dying by the thousands and the Americans will probably follow suit.

All of a sudden, all the girls' eyes looked at one place, at George. The sun was shining on his face and the girls were drooling. They all were saying, in silence "WOW." To them he was the best-looking man they have ever seen. His uniform was for a corporal but who cares. The girls just wanted him to, survive and take them to America.

CHAPTER 8

─────── ❁ ───────

Haskell, Kansas

Doctor Guest and his wife Rebecca were overwhelmed with patients. People from other towns came by foot, horse, wagon, and car to see him. He was the only doctor still well enough to help treat those with this new disease that was killing so many. Most of the dead were the young but everyone was affected. So many people came to him too late to be treated and with limited supplies he was hard pressed to give any treatment at all. His yard was overflowing with the sick, the dying and the dead. At his age he thought that he and Rebecca would be able to savor whatever time they had left but it was not to be. He could not even bury the dead because he had no time to even treat the living.

Rebecca was helping but she was not well either; besides, what could she do? Some of the best hospitals back east could not handle this "Spanish Flu" so how could she and Jonathon?

"Rebecca, how are you feeling today?"

"Not much better Jonathon." she said.

"I don't know what we will do with the dead outside." "Who will help us bury them?"

"Johathon, we need to concentrate on us now." "We are no good to anyone if we get sick."

"As usual you are right Rebecca."

As the wife suggested to the doctor, Jonathon and her washed often, wore a mask, and changed clothes and washed them every day. So far it is working to keep them well.

CHAPTER 9

— ❂ —

Haskell, County 3/10/1917

The winter of 1917-18 was one of the coldest on history east of the Rockies. Rebecca has been together with her husband for 46 good years where they raised a good son and cared for many friends and other sick people. With 13 years with the Guests their dog Spot, could not stay outside anymore because of the weather. In a way that was a good thing because the dog would join his owners under the covers at night.

Rebecca was the first one to die from the flu at 78, a good age for the time. Johnaton follows at 75 a day later. They had a long, good life with many friends and patients They leave behind a son, in name only, Peter and their dog, Spot, named because of all the black spots on his coat. Spot has been a member of the family for 13 years and now he lays at the foot of their bed to keep them company and watch over their bodies. A neighbor comes by to see if there is anyone at home and if they are ok, sees the two bodies and the dog and kills Spot. Dogs were considered a source of the epidemic and many were killed on mass by police and others. Peter is now alone, not knowing that he has a brother. Because of how important the Guests are, the town found two caskets for them and buried them and Spot in their back yard.

CHAPTER 10

—✦— ❂ —✦—

Haskel Kansas 1917

Peter had just turned 17 and he could easily pass for 18 or more. He had no parents and even his dog was dead; he had only himself. He did have an idea to go to war and find a new life and new people, he might even find love but, he had already found love with Sara. Peter was not a 'good boy" because he and Sara fooled around and unknown to either of them, she was pregnant. Sara did feel a little strange but she attributed it to the flu. Peter and Sara did talk about him joining the army before he turns 18 and he must join. Sara was a pretty woman and a good writer so if Peter joins up, she will try to get a job with a newspaper. Another option was for Peter to wait until he turns 18 and maybe the war would be over. He could still live in his parent's house, but he made up his mind, he wanted to go now. If he knew that Sara was pregant that might change his mind but, he did not know.

Now that his parents and even his dog were gone, he did not know what to do. With only Sara to love and with no prospects Peter decided to join the army and fight. He had no hatred for Germany but it just seemed something to do. It gave him a chance to see Europe and with a high school diploma and after training he might be made an officer. He also had some medical training from his father and that could also help get a high officer position in the service. He was not sure what branch to enter because he heard that there was a high percent of fliers that die in battle and he did not want to die that way. Trench was also bad because of the mustard gas so; he might go into artillery. Those big guns make a lot of noise and with no ear protection you can go deaf. Maybe he could buy heavy muffs of some kind and wear them do would do his best to train to use the deadly weapons. There is also the chance that he may try to fly.

CHAPTER 11

Camp Funston

People from Haskell carried influenza to Camp Funston.

Sam and Howard both have finished their three-month training, just like Peter and all three will have to go to a formal camp for more training before they get on a ship and sail to France.

Camp Funston is a U.S. Army training camp located on Fort Riley, southwest of Manhattan, Kansas. The camp was named for Brigadier General Frederick Funston (1865–1917). It is one of sixteen such camps established at the outbreak of World War 1. Severe influenza was raging in Haskell in Feb 1918. In 3 weeks, 1,100 troops got sick. Peter was assigned to this camp as well as his two friends Sam and Howard. Because of Peter's medical experience he helped with the sick.

During World War I, Camp Funston also served as a detention camp for conscientious objectors (COs) many of which were Mennonite in faith. Since it was compulsory, Hutterites sent their young men to military camps, but they did not allow them to obey any military commands or wear a uniform.

Sam and Howard were in the same camp but they had little time to see each other. Because of Peter's education and medical work with his father, he was made a first lieutenant while, Sam was made a corporal and Howard was made a sergeant. All three will have men to lead.

Peter had gotten sick on the train to camp and his face was still pale. Army food was just as bad as he had heard and he did not think he could eat anyway. The train was noisy, smelly, and lacking in any normal sanitation. The other soldiers were making all kinds of animal noises with their body parts. He could not believe that these soldiers were going to represent America to Europe.

The camp has many people from his home town, Haskell. The training involved; learning military procedures, who to salute, etc. The use of a rifle because very few of the recruits knew how to shot and how to use the bayonet for close combat; the officers also learned to use a pistol but, the main weapon would be the rifle. Peter was made a first lieutenant because of his education and medical work. He was happy and proud for the silver bar on his uniform and he wished his parents could see it.

CHAPTER 12

Train to New York

The recruits from Camp Funston were far from New York and the train trip took hours. This gave the train and recruits plenty of time to stink like wild animals. The food was eatable and plenty of it so, the recruits ate up because they did not know what to expect on the ship. The train was very noisy and the smoke from the train, and people smoking, made it almost impossible to sleep. Sanitary was a hole in the floor but, at least there was a door for some privacy. This war is terrible already an it has not even started yet.

By the time the train arrived in New York all the troops wanted to do was go back home. If the train was this bad the ship will be worse because there was the possibility of being attacked by the Germans and the American ship only carried troops and packed weapons.

CHAPTER 13

——— ✱ ———

Cruise to Franch\e

The ship was worse than Peter could imagine. The largest ship he was ever in before was a rowboat that he could catch small fish from. He thought of those days now and he wondered why he had left that behind for the unknown. He had never left Kansas and now he was to fight in what was being called a World War or the "War to End All Wars." On this ship, Leviathan and other ships, troops were quarantined and soldiers were sealed into separate areas behind closed doors. Portholes were shut because of fear of submarines. With no room for the sick the sick were layered on decks. Dead were buried at sea. Leviathan would transport 100k troops to Europe but, this trip, it held more.

There was so much blood all over the ship that no matter where you walked you had to track it to other places on the ship. Peter had a lot of medical training therefore he was elected to help care for the sick He could have stayed home instead of this trip. The Levithan was a large ship that had made this voyage before and would make it again unless the ship, is attacked by the Germans.

Germany had made mistakes that forced America's hand and now they may pay the price.

CHAPTER 14

New York to Brest part 2

After a trip, that was filled with sick soldiers who were upchucking or nauseous, or some other illness including many with the flu they could see land that may be France and the end of the trip.

40% of the two million American troops who arrived in France disembarked at Brest. Because it was a deep-water port many ships could disembark simultaneously. Troops from all over the world disembarked at Brest.

Marie, as well as other girls in town were watching the American soldiers disembark and she could not believe how sick they were from the trip but, she did see one soldier with an officer pin and he was the most handsome man that she has ever seen. But then she realized that she had seen him from another ship but he was a corporal. How can that be? What a lost if he were to die. She noticed that he was looking at her but, in a different way as the other soldiers did. The other soldiers and other men looked at her with only one thing on their mind and that scared her but, this new officer looked at her with kindness as if he was sorry for the horror she must endure. She wanted to meet him or them. Is it possible that there are two men that beautiful, maybe twins. All she could think is dirty thoughts, like how she would like to be the meat in that sandwich. She did not want either one to be wounded so she could meet one, but how else could she. Thet were given orders not to talk with the soldiers unless they were wounded. What a stupid order.

CHAPTER 15

Army Air Force

Rickenbacker was a race car driver before joining the United States Army in 1917 when America entered World War I. He was sent to France with the rank of sergeant with the desire to fly planes. When he met Col. Billy Mitchell, an aviation pioneer, who saw him reassigned to the new Army Air Corps.

Rickenbacker took out his first enemy aircraft on April 29, 1918, with many more to come. Within his first month flying, he shot down five German planes, making him an "Ace" in the Air Force, also earning him the French *Croix de Guerre*.

In just nine months, he shot down a total of 26 enemy planes where he became an "Ace of Aces," simultaneously earning him the Distinguished Service Cross on seven occasions. Furthermore, he also received the Medal of Honor, making him one of the most decorated American in World War One and a legend in the Air Force.

Peter had heard about Rickenbacker and he wanted to be just like him. With some training, Peter was allowed to fly. He found right away how dangerous flying these bi-planes were. Every day pilots on both sides, are being shot down and killed. Peter had two "kills" before he was shot down. He was able to land what was left of his plane and survive his wounds. He landed on his side of the no man's line and was saved by soldiers on his side, one that he knew from training, Howard. Howard was not in the air force as a flyer but a mechanic; someone needed to help keep the planes flying.

Peter was wounded in the crash and was driven by ambulance to a camp hospital.

Leonard learned to fly and he also met a friend that also liked men and liked boys. Even though this was France, they had to keep that a secret as best as they could. The other man, called Mark, was a medium tall, dark-haired man of 20. He had experienced that Leonard did not have but, Leonard wanted to learn. He was not as handsome as George but he will do especially because George will never join the crew. Unknow to Leonard George's twin was also here before he was shot down. He would really get excited if he knew there were two of them.

Leonard was able to get three "kills" before he was shot down and when he went to the hospital, he got the shock of his life.

CHAPTER 16

Haskel, Kansas

The pains that Sara was experiencing were getting worse and needed a visit to a doctor which is difficult to do because their office is filled with flu patients so, Sara took a pain killer but that was no help. After several weeks sara's mother told her that she was probably having a baby and who is the father. Since the only man she was with was Peter, he had to be the father. By now he was half way to France in a ship and he does not know he was going to be a father and if he would survive long enough to see his son or daughter.

Because Sara was good in English and writing she found a writer's job at the local newspaper. It was a dream job but, now that she was expecting she would have to give up the job.

CHAPTER 17

Field Hospital in France

Jack had seen battles before and he had been wounded before, that is how he met the beautiful aide, Marie, his sister in the hospital as he recovered. Jack had not met many women but none as beautiful as his sister. If there was no war, she would have the men in line to date her.

This time Jack was wounded more seriously and when he recovers, he will be sent home as unfit for battle. Jack did his job defending his country, received three medals, and his parents will be happy to have him back. Jack will wear those medals with pride and they would help with the single women.

It was nice to talk to a friend from home, Howard. Peter's injuries were not too serious but, they were serious enough that he needed a stay at the hospital. While in the hospital they saw an angel, Marie. Peter had seen her while getting off the troop ship and he could never forget that face. Howard had never seen her before but when he first saw her, it was like being hit with a thunder bolt. It looks like Marie has two more suiters but, of these two she knows who she likes best.

Since he was wounded, she could talk to him, and she did.

"Do you speak any French, soldier? "She said.

"A little" he said.

"Are you the officer or the corporal?" she said.

Peter was confused, "I am a lieutenant, who is the corporal?"

"I saw you get off one ship and the corporal get off another. You must be identical twins."

Now Peter understood. He always had a feeling that he was not complete and that he had a brother somewhere and now he knows. How can he have a brother and not know about it?

Marie sat down and started a conversation with him. She asked all kinds of questions such as, his name, where he is from, and the big one, does he have a girlfriend back home and she did not like the answer to that. They were both surprised at how easy it was to talk to each other. They both noticed that the other wounded soldiers were looking at them and they were jealous. Peter was surprised that she wanted to talk to him and not any other soldiers, but he was not complaining..

Peter asked her questions too. He asked her name, about her family and, if she had a boyfriend, he liked the answer to that, and especially why she became a nurse. Peter loved the answer to that question as well, "Because she wanted to help." He knew that if he was not with Sara that he would fall in love with her. He did not know that she was already in love with him.

And then Leonard was wheeled in and saw Peter. Leonard was quickly wheeled over to Peter and Marie and yelled out "George". But it was not George. Now all three of them started to talk about George and Peter about himself. They laughed at meeting like this and both being shot down and serving in the air. Peter now knows who his brother is and who he wants to meet before one of them gets killed.

CHAPTER 18

———— ❁ ————

Patton and the Tank Corp

Juan was a sergeant and knew how to drive a car so, he was able to get training with a tank and he worked under Patton and saw how he worked and how brave he was.

Patton's efficiency as a tank commander won him promotion to lieutenant colonel, but he worried the war would end before he had a chance to lead his tankers in combat. That chance came at Saint Mihiel on 12 September 1918. Unsurprisingly, he didn't stay at his command post but roamed the field under fire, directing attacks; his tankers did well and showed plenty of fighting spirit.

He had been chastised for leaving his command post during the battle at Saint-Mihiel, but he did the same during the Meuse-Argonne Offensive. He followed his tanks into combat, even helping to dig a path for them through two trenches While attempting to lead a unit of pinned-down infantry against the Germans, he was shot through the leg but continued to direct the attack. He wrote to his wife from his hospital bed on 12 October 1918, saying, "Peace looks possible, but I rather hope not for I would like to have a few more fights. They are awfully thrilling like steeple chasing only more so." He was promoted to colonel. The Armistice came on his thirty-third birthday. All in all, Patton had had a quite satisfactory war.

CHAPTER 19

Third Battle of Ypres: July 31 to November 6, 1917

Also known as the Third Battle of Ypres, takes place in Ypres, Belgium, as British forces, with help from the French and the use of tanks, launch an attack to wrest control of Ypres from the Germans. Attacks and counterattacks ensue for four months in the rain and mud, with Canadian forces brought in to help relieve the troops but little ground being won. In the end, it is considered a victory for the Allies, with but one that costs both sides more than 550,000 casualties. Archie was wounded again and sent to a camp hospital to be repaired. This was his second wound and second medal, one more wound and he can go home. He wanted to go home but, he did not want to be shot again.

CHAPTER 20

──── ✳ ────

Meuse-Argonne Offensive

The Meuse-Argonne offensive was massive and consisted of 15 divisions, 600,000 men, 3,000 pieces of artillery, and 90,000 horses.

This was the largest action in American military history until then. The battle started in the last half of October and caused 117,000 American casualties in 47 days. Two brothers from San Antonio were wounded at the same battle, Steven, and Jose. Both survived and for their other brother, Juan this was his third battle and he received another medal to brag about. This was the first and only time that three brothers were wounded at the same battle. Rather than have this happen again and maybe have all three brothers killed, all three went to a hospital and sent home as heroes. This happened again in World War 2 when the five Sullivan brothers were all killed when their ship was sunk.

This was the Meuse-Argon offensive. It produces the so-called Lost Battalion. They were trapped for 5 days and suffered 70% causalities. It had Alvin York who captured 132 Germans in one day.

CHAPTER 21

Truman in Battle

He saw his first action in August 1918, amid the mud and mire of the Vosges mountain range in Alsace-Lorraine, firing an artillery barrage and being fired on in return. The captain stood his ground. Many of his men did not. He cursed them for it, and won their respect.

Forced marches in cold, bitter rain brought them to the Argonne Forest and the enormous offensive that would end the war. Truman remembered that the opening barrage, to which his battery contributed, belched out "more noise than human ears could stand. Men serving the guns became deaf for weeks after. Some were deaf as a post from the noise. It looked as though every gun in France was turned loose and the sky was red from one end to the other from the artillery flashes. The artillery followed the infantry, and at the end of it all, with the armistice in November, only one man in Truman's battery, Battery D, had been killed in action and only two others had been wounded, all of them while detailed to another command. He had performed exceptionally well. The war was the making of him.

CHAPTER 22

Battle of Cantigny (May 27 – June 5, 1918)

The first full battle by the U.S. forces in World War One, and the first American offensive against the Germans. The Battle of Belleau Wood (June 1-26, 1918)-U.S. Army and Marine Corps troops engaged the Germans.

Because the Americans did not have them in sufficient quantity, the French provided air cover, 368 heavy artillery pieces, trench mortars, tanks, and flamethrowers. The French tanks were from the French 5th Tank Battalion. Their primary purpose was to eliminate German machine gun positions. With this massive support, and advancing on schedule behind the creeping artillery barrage, the 28th Infantry took the village in 30 minutes. It then continued to its final objective roughly a half kilometer beyond the village.

Sam and Howard were both involved with this battel, Sam in infantry and Howard by fixing planes so they can contribute to the battle. Sam survived the battle with a medal and Howard received one for his ability to keep the plans in the air. Most senior offices believe that the Germans are ready to give up. It was the addition of the Americas that turned the tide. The fresh soldiers helped with keeping up French moral.

CHAPTER 23

Battle of Belleau Wood

Fought between June 6 and June 26, 1918, where the US Marines earned the nickname "Devil Dogs" for their fierce fighting.

Although George was not a marine he still fought at the battle and once again was wounded This makes number three so he can go home, which he does want to do until he saw the most beautiful woman he ever saw while being treated for his new wounds

CHAPTER 24

Field Hospital, Franch

And so, they met, George, Peter, and Marie. It was quite a shock to see the twins meet for the first time. Marie could not choose which one was better looking because they were identical. The only way she could tell the difference were the stripes on his sleeves. It seems as if he got a promotion, which is not a surprise with all the battles he was in that he now has four stripes. When Peter looked at George it was like looking at a mirror.

The two brothers asked all types of questions such as who are you, where are from, who are your parents, any more brothers, or sisters. Marie listened carefully because she wanted to know the answers. The one question that she wanted the answer to was "Do you have a girlfriend back home." and George lied and said "No." Savana would disagree, but George was hit by love. Marie did not know if he was lying because it was impossible for someone that looked like him could not have a girlfriend but she accepted the answer.

Now that George heard her talk, he loved the sound of her voice. He wonders if he had a chance with her. She must have a dozen boyfriends, but he did have a chance. Marie knew that Peter had someone back home so she had no chance with him although she probably could change his mind, George was another thing. She could tell that George was interested in her, everyone was. So maybe she could settle for the sergeant instead. After all, they were the same; they even sounded the same.

As so, they started long conversations. George wanted her and wanted to knew what she felt about America, did she ever think of moving to America? She told him that everyone wanted to go to America and she wanted to knew if he wanted to move to France and he said "not really." Since he did not have to go to battle, he was able to see Marie, when she was available and she tried to be available as often as possible. They ate meals together and one night they kissed for the first time and it was like magic. After that first kiss, they both knew that they wanted to be together so, it was time to meet the parents.

Marie was able to take a leave and travel to her home and see her family again, but this time she went with George. Her father w impressed with George's three battle medals and three wound medals. George was happy to meet the family and even more happy that they all spoke some English. Many countries in Europe teach English in school. The family wanted to talk about his battles and how he survived them. They thanked him for fighting for France. They asked about Texas and can he ride a house and he told them about Shorty. He also told them about his twin brother who he did not even know that he had. The first thing he is going to do when he gets back is ask about his brother. Then he asked, "the question" can he marry Marie and take her to Texas?

The family was surprised at the question but they though it might be a good idea. France was wrecked by the war and needed to work on the buildings and roads that were destroyed. This would not be a good place to raise a new family. Marie was sorry about leaving her home but it will be fun to start her own family in a new country.

CHAPTER 25

Peace

It is said that a war will end when one side has enough. Germany and it's allies have had enough. The large influx of American troops was more than Germany could endure. It became obvious that they had lost too many men and their moral was poor. The war was over because Germany lost their will to fight.

ARMISTICE 11/11/1918

The Armistice of 11 November 1918 ended World War 1, the "Wat that ends all Wars". But it wasn't. The total number of military and civilian casualties in World War I was about 40 million: estimates range from around 15 to 22 million deaths and about 23 million wounded who were left disfigured by bullets and gas attacks.

Many military personnel, ranking it among the deadliest conflicts in human history.

Besides the millions killed in the war, there was additional consequences such as:

- The kingdoms of Austria and Hungary were separated and established as independent nations, while three new nation-states were formed: Czechoslovakia, Poland, and Yugoslavia.
- Russia become a communist country. The Russian Revolution caused the communist to come to power and helped create the environment for the Korean and Vietnam wars.
- The reparations forced on Germany at the peace talks destroyed the economy of Germany and its citizens, The price of a loaf of bread could cost a week's salary, if there were any jobs to be had. The poverty of Germany made it easy for Hitler to come to power.
- Japan was enraged that their work in the war was not rewarded and they were not treated as an equal.

EPILOGUE

WWI was a terrible event with millions dying. It was basically caused by hatred. There were 38 people in this book and it was difficult to decide who would live, who would die, and who, if anyone would get to be with the beautiful young French nurse. I decided to list who is left and what is their future. I hope you agree with my choices.

The war affected many people in many countries.

- Sara had a beautiful girl that she and Peter came home to enjoy. He did not forget Marie, when he was in bed with Sara, he fantasized about Marie.
- Leonard recovered from the crash injuries and stayed in France with his friend where they were welcome. His parents did not understand but, they were glad that he was alive.
- Sam and Howard both returned to Kansas with no wounds but with two battle medals. There were some people from Haskell who did not return and several came back as a cripple, war is hell.
- Pierre survived at home, working at the military office, logging the names of injured and dead. He was the first to know the names of the town's wounded and killed.
- Jack went back home and was just as glad to see his family, as they were to see him. After a rest he would go back to the dock, easily found work as well as a nice lady who he dated, married, and had two girls with beautiful blond hair.
- Bridget did meet someone else to date. They married and had two sons who fought in WW 2 and were killed during a V2 rocket attack while on leave in London.
- The process to see if Father John becomes a saint is continuing. There was one certified miracle attributed to him.

- George came back to San Antonio with his beautiful bride who was 2 months pregnant with a beautify set of twins, one girl and one boy. They did take a ship back to France so that her family could see her and the twins.
- Peter made a trip to San Antonio to see his brother's family and think how things could be different. He talked to George's parents and discovered how he and George were split up.
- Archie went home to Amanda with his 2 battle medals wan 2 wound medals. Amanda would have three girls which pleased Archie because they would not have to fight in any war.
- Nora recovered from losing Noah but, did not find anyone to take his place, she did become a teacher in early grades and taught the students how to paint. She did not have a lover but, she loves the children.

REFERENCES

No book that involves historical characters and events could be accurately portrayed without the use of references. Although I tried to make this book as factual as possible it is after all a novel and I did need to take allowances for the stake of the story.

The following are some of the references that I used to write this book. In addition, I used the Internet extensively. In cases where the reader believes that accuracy is in doubt, it is the fault of the author and not the source.

- Cooke, David C. Sky Battles 1914-1918 The Story of Aviation in WWI. W. W. Norton & Co. NY, 1970.
- Byron Farwell, Over There, – The U.S. In The Great War 1917-1918, 1999, W.W. Norton and Co, Inc.
- Stephen Hunter and John Bainbridge, American Gunfight The Plot to Kill Harry Truman – And the Shootout That Stopped it. Simon & Schuster NY 2005
- Trevor Nevit Dupup Col., U.S. Army, retired, The Military History of World War I The War in the Air Franklin Watts Inc, NY, London, 1976
- Richard Holmes, The Western Front, 1999 TV Books L.L.C. NY, NY 10019
- David McCullough, Truman Simon & Schuster N.Y. 1992
- National Geographic, Tracking the Next Killer Flu, October 2005, Vol 208 #4, pp 2-31
- Persico, Joseph E. The Great Swine Flu Epidemic of 1918, American heritage 27 (June 1976): 28-31, 80-85.
- The Great Influenza: The Epic Story of the Deadliest Plague in History, Viking Penguin Press, N.Y., N.Y. 10014, 2004

Other books by the author
Non-Fiction

- *Teaching Computers in Pre-K Through 8th Grade*
- *The Art of Bridget*
- *Conversation With Myself. A life Well Lived*

Fiction

- *Succession*
- *TLC*

Look for the authors next book, the start of a series of murders that happen at famous places. The first being, *Murder at Macys*.

Printed in the United States
by Baker & Taylor Publisher Services